CHILDHOOD SWEETHEARTS V

JACOB SPEARS

GOOD2GO PUBLISHING

Childhood Sweethearts V
Written by Jacob Spears
Cover design: Davida Baldwin
Typesetter: Mychea
ISBN: 978-1-943686-59-9

Copyright ©2016 Good2Go Publishing
Published 2016 by Good2Go Publishing
7311 W. Glass Lane • Laveen, AZ 85339
www.good2gopublishing.com
https://twitter.com/good2gobooks
G2G@good2gopublishing.com
www.facebook.com/good2gopublishing
www.instagram.com/good2gopublishing

ACKNOWLEDGEMENTS

I'd like to acknowledge my mother, Lenora Sarantos; my sisters, Amy McKinney, Heather Hopkins, and Tabatha Potter; and my brothers, Chris Hopkins and Leon Hopkins. I'd like to thank Emmett Leon Hopkins. Thank you for raising me as your own and for teaching me how to be a man.

I'd also like to acknowledge Lt. Bettineschi, Sgt. Joseph, Novoa, Ollis, Landi, Guin, Spencer, and Cranmer—and if I left you out, I'm sorry.

Last but not least, I want to shout out to Trayvon D. Jackson, a.k.a. Sue Rabbit. To our empire!

"We win some, we lose some. So, let every move you make, and every decision you contemplate, be made prudently."

~Trayvon D. Jackson, Author

1

ROXY GOT OUT of bed exhausted from being up all night with Sue Rabbit. When she looked over at him, he was sound asleep. She smiled.

This man is blowing my mind, Roxy thought.

She checked the clock. It was 5:45 a.m. She had to be at the restaurant to open at 6:30 a.m. So Roxy strutted from the bedroom and hopped into the hot, steaming yet soothing shower. In the shower, she thought of how fortunate she was to still have Sue Rabbit as a free man in spite of all the DEA sweeps that occurred two months ago. She felt sorry for Smooth, who was being held in federal housing at the Martin County Jail.

Damn, Smooth! Roxy thought while washing her curly locks.

Since Smooth's arrest, China hadn't been to work, and Roxy clearly understood her pain.

I just hope he gets a good deal, because federal prison is no joke. Them bitches want you 100 percent of their time, Roxy reflected. *Damn, Smooth! Why did you have to get yourself fucked up?*

When Roxy stepped out of the shower, she wrapped herself in a towel and walked back into the room to prepare herself for work. Sue Rabbit was in a coma-like sleep and never stirred as she got dressed. When she was all set to go, she gave him a kiss on his lips and then sauntered out of their bedroom and off to work.

* * *

Amanda couldn't stop crying her eyes out for Smooth. She wrote to him every day, praying and hoping that he would prevail over his situation. It was evident that someone had ratted him out. She just wished she knew who it was. Lately she had been having constant headaches and now was stuck on the toilet at 6:25 a.m. with diarrhea.

"What the fuck is wrong with me?" she strained out while holding onto her stomach.

I need to go see a damn doctor about this, Amanda thought while spinning toilet paper from a roll to wipe her ass.

She then hopped in the shower and thought about Smooth, just like she did 24/7.

"Damn, baby! Please come home!" Amanda cried out, falling to the floor of the shower, entrapped in another one of her moments of missing Smooth.

She couldn't believe that someone had set him up. He was too careful and very observant when trafficking, yet still someone had managed to infiltrate him.

After Amanda had pulled herself together and gotten out of the shower, she put on some clothes and sat at her kitchen table to write Smooth another letter. It was the only tool that kept her mind level when she had one of her moments.

* * *

"Guru! Stop playing so much," Landi said, trying her best to escape his tickling.

He had her pinned to the bed, tickling her underneath her armpits.

"Baby! Stop! Okay!" she cried out, with tears in her eyes and on the edge of pissing on herself.

"So, we good, right?"

"Yes, Guru. We are good," Landi yielded.

"No more sneak attacks!"

"No more sneak attacks, baby."

"Promise?" Guru asked.

"Promise, baby!" Landi answered.

Guru raised up off of Landi and finished getting dressed to go meet with Sue Rabbit. When he had received the call, they had just finished making love. Landi cast a fit when he agreed to leave.

She didn't want Guru to be out on the streets, especially after the sweep and learning that the DEA was upset for not getting Juan José before someone killed him and his lover. The DEA was even more furious knowing that Mario Lopez was still alive and somewhere hiding. Although the incident occurred two months ago, it was way too early for Guru to be stepping back out.

"Baby, please. Don't do what I think you're about to do!" Landi spoke, hugging her pillow to her bare breasts.

"And what do you think is on my mind, baby?" Guru asked while checking the clip in his Glock .22 before placing it in the waistband of his jeans.

"You're about to start back hustling. I heard you talking to Sue Rabbit the other day."

"Why are you so worried, baby? The DEA don't know shit 'bout me and Sue Rabbit. So the risk of being caught up is slim," Guru explained.

"I just don't want to lose you, Guru," Landi purred, with tears forming in her eyes. "Just let it go before someone gives you up," Landi replied, unable to stop the tears from falling.

Guru walked over to her and wrapped her in a warming embrace. He then kissed her on the lips.

"I'ma be alright, and like I told you, this will end soon."

"Promise me?" Landi sniffled.

"I promise, baby. Just give me a lil time to make sure my boy is situated."

"Okay. I will do that. I love you, Guru."

"I love you too, baby," Guru responded.

* * *

Mario was a smart man to relocate, since he was wanted in Miami. He was now shacked up in Ft. Lauderdale with one of his baby mamas, Tasha. She was a beautiful black woman who stood five three, weighed 125 pounds, and had a Coke-bottle frame. She was a model for *Smooth Magazine*. She was happy to have Mario back in her life for the sake of their six-year-old son, who looked just like Mario. However, Mario looked like a completely different person now. He grew out his hair and had a full beard, whereas he used to be clean-shaven, including his head.

Despite the heat, he was still able to push dope on the blocks that he and Juan had controlled. The M-13s who were back on the streets acknowledged their new leader with mad respect. Mario was on a mission. He wanted retaliation for the death of Juan. He knew that Smooth was behind the hit, but the last thing he would ever expect was for China to be the assassin. Still, he was out to get her because she was now up for grabs, being that Smooth was incarcerated. Mario was sitting in the den of Tasha's beautiful home, smoking a phat blunt of kush with Javier while watching *Dancing with the Stars*.

"Yo, homes! Amber Rose has a big-ass booty!" Javier said, taking a swig of his Bud Light.

"Yeah, she do! Too much for you, homes?"

"Shit! Who you take me for, a mini-me?" Javier stated.

4

"Come on, homes. You can't handle that shit! Look at her!" Mario said while pointing at Amber Rose on the sixty-four-inch flat-screen television.

"I think you're talking about yourself, esé!" Javier joked as he puffed on the blunt before passing it back to Mario.

Mario grabbed the blunt, took a puff, and turned the volume down to zero.

"So what's the news on China, second man in command?" Mario asked Javier, who was now second behind the M-13s.

"No one has seen her. I even have men watching the restaurant, and still no one sees her," Javier explained.

"And she's no longer at the apartment?"

"Nope!"

"Where do you think she's hiding?" Mario asked.

"My guess would be that she's somewhere close to Smooth."

"Maybe she is, homes. So we have to do a little more soul searching," Mario considered.

"What are you considering?" Javier asked.

"We have a couple brothers in Martin County who we need to get in contact with," Mario suggested.

"Juan loved you for a reason. Now I see why, homie. You're too intelligent to fail!" Javier said.

"Follow my lead, esé, and you will become just like your big brother," Mario said, rubbing the top of Javier's head.

2

"MA. I PROMISE I will be over to see you once I get back in town," China told GaGa over the phone.

China was living in the $2.3 million mansion that Smooth had purchased before he was apprehended by the feds. No one but Roxy, GaGa, and her girls, Jane and Tabby, knew where she was living.

Her surprise pregnancy was exciting to everyone, including herself. She was gladsome of becoming a mother, just as much as everyone else around her was. Her girlfriends were already showering her with baby gifts before even knowing the gender of the two-month-old baby she was carrying. She didn't find out the gender.

"China, when you come to town, I better be the first person on your list to see, or we gonna have problems, Miss Thang!" GaGa promised.

"Yes, Mom. I got you. I promise I will be over as soon as I get back in town."

"Okay, baby. Call me when you do. Mama loves you."

"I love you too, Mom," China replied as she then hung up her iPhone 6.

"Lord, everyone's killing me with this extra concern shit! Like they never seen a pregnant woman before?" China expressed to herself and Zorro, who was lying on top of her coverlet on her and Smooth's king-sized bed—a bed she couldn't wait to share with him again.

Some nights she'd sit up and rub her stomach thinking about how they would be as a family.

With him looking at federal time, I have no idea how long he'll be gone, especially in Martin County, also known as Ku Klux Klan Town, China thought as she prepared to take a road trip to go visit Smooth and then Jenny.

Her girl, Jenny, was super excited to be a stepmother and couldn't wait for the baby to come. But she, like China, hated that she would miss out on three years of the baby's life. *Don't worry, baby girl. I'll name the baby after you too,* China thought as she placed her neatly folded clothes into her suitcase.

She then opened her nightstand drawer and removed her Glock .45. She checked the clip and saw that it was full, so she placed it into her Prada handbag. China was always ready to handle business. She now had to care for more than herself; there were two lives—hers and the baby's.

When China saw that she had everything ready for her road trip. She picked up her phone and called Miranda. The phone rang twice before Miranda picked up.

"Hi, Miranda. Sorry to bother you, but are you busy this weekend?" China asked.

"No, China. I'm doing the same thing I do every weekend. Let me guess. You're going to see Smooth, and Zorro wants to come over," Miranda stated, already knowing why China was calling her.

"Well, yes. I'm going to see him, and Zorro does want to see his godmother," China joked while looking at the dog, whose ears were erect at the mention of his name.

"Bring him over, because I could do for some company."

"Okay!"

"See you soon. And are you staying healthy for the baby?"

"Yes, I am," China replied.

"That's wonderful! See you soon," Miranda said before hanging up the phone.

"Come on, Zorro! You're going to your godmother's house while I go visit Daddy," China said as she grabbed Zorro's leash from behind the bedroom door.

Zorro ran up to her and allowed her to snap on the leash. China then gripped the leash, grabbed her suitcase, and rolled it down the staircase with Zorro in tow. When she stepped outside, the sun licked at her skin.

"Damn! It's hot out here today! This would be a great day to hit the beach!" China said to Zorro as she placed him in the backseat of her new all-black Mercedes-Benz SUV.

She was about to hop into the driver's seat, until she remembered that she had forgotten to set the house alarm. She returned to the house, entered the five-digit passcode, and walked back to the car and started it up.

"Here we come, Daddy!" China said as she pulled out of the driveway on her way to Miranda's.

* * *

"Man, we need to see what Smooth is gonna do. Shit! We still have the blocks ready to eat again," Sue Rabbit said to Guru, who had come over to Sue and Roxy's condo.

"It's kinda hard to inform him of anything when the feds might be listening to everything we say," Guru said.

"Man, I still think that China could help us out, bro."

"Yeah, me too. Let's not forget the soldier did a bid herself for holding down the team with her man," Guru added.

"Yeah, and now it's time to see if she'll help out the team, stay aboard."

"She's anti-drug association, and this is before Smooth fell. It's what broke them apart in the first place!" Guru said, taking a bit from his egg sandwich that Sue had cooked up for both of them.

"I say we wait until he calls again. We'll then bring it to him in the best lingo we can without tipping off the feds," Sue Rabbit suggested. "Meantime, we got a hundred kilos to get cooked up. At least I know who will handle it for us, and we won't have to kill her afterward."

Guru agreed with Sue by chewing and shaking his head.

"That sounds good. Before you know it, word will be out that we're back on!"

"And before the feds come snooping, we'll both have enough to retire. We can't go for the all-timers. We have to just get us and get out, bro!" Sue added as he bit into his sandwich with gusto.

Guru felt good knowing that Sue Rabbit also wanted to back out of the game and not be acquisitive. He knew the cost of being greedy and moving without a set goal. It was a risk they were about to take, and they were both aware.

But every chance is a risk, Guru thought.

"Let's just pray that China will help us stay aboard," Guru said.

"Yeah, right!" Sue Rabbit replied.

* * *

Since Banga's death, Meka was devastated and still in her own world. It wasn't the same, and the drought on the streets he provided for spoke for itself. When she saw Smooth's face appear on the news, it hurt her more than losing Banga.

Today, Meka decided to step out of her grief shell and unexpectedly go visit Smooth. When she pulled up to the Martin County Jail, she checked her makeup in the visor mirror. She dug into her purse and pulled out her lip liner to accentuate her crimson lipstick and sprayed on some Beyoncé Pulse perfume.

"Okay, girl. You killin' 'em!" she complimented herself.

When she stepped out of her champagne Lexus, she adjusted her miniskirt that had climbed up her lustrous thighs. As Meka walked toward the front door, she turned heads from all directions.

"Damn, lil momma. What's up?" a sideline hustler who was visiting his baby mama asked Meka.

Meka ignored the hustler and continued on her way.

When she got inside and stepped up to the receptionist, she popped a bubble and then spoke up. "I'm here to visit inmate Donavan Johnson," Meka said, smacking on her bubblegum, which irritated the receptionist.

"Give us a moment, ma'am," the receptionist said through the mic while she looked up Smooth's location on the computer.

"Okay. Booth 17. He'll be there shortly, ma'am."

"Thank you," Meka said as she strutted into the visiting area where other friends and family were spending time with their loved ones.

When Smooth stepped into the chatty atmosphere, he was expecting to see China—and certainly not Meka.

Damn! She's about to block China from coming today! Smooth thought as he sat down and put the phone to his ear.

"What's up, Meka?" he said calmly, trying not to reveal the discontent of seeing her just pop up after his two months of incarceration.

"Hi, baby! I hope you're not mad at me for not coming sooner, but I really needed to get myself together after Banga's funeral," Meka said, trying her best not to break down in front of him. *The last thing Smooth needs is a weak bitch by his side*, Meka thought. "It's just not the same without him," she added.

"It's okay, Meka. I can understand what you're going through. It's good to see you too, beautiful," Smooth said, licking his lips like Meka loved to see him do.

He took notice of how gorgeous she looked. She was definitely fly. Her hair was done in finger waves, her nails were freshly painted, and she had on a V-shaped blouse revealing the fact that she was not wearing a bra. Smooth could see her erect nipples protruding through.

"I miss you, Smooth. How the fuck did this happen? I've been trying to figure this shit out forever. They need to let you go like Ham. Shit! He's free now!"

"Say what?" Smooth exclaimed, giving Meka a sharp stare.

"Yeah, boo. Ham is home. They dropped all his charges two weeks ago," Meka informed him.

For two months, Smooth had been trying to see where he had gone wrong. For a fact, he knew that someone had ratted him out, and it was someone who knew that he would be meeting with Banga to do the drop at Rimes Food Market. The only ones close enough were Amanda and Ham.

Oh shit! Ham! It gotta be him. Who the fuck posts a million-dollar bond without help? Smooth thought.

"Meka! Ham's bond was a million dollars. You mean to tell me that all his charges got dropped?"

"Yes, boo. He came home two weeks ago. I thought he was looking at bricks, baby," Meka said, reckoning the same prospect Smooth was now thinking, from the hint in her voice.

"Meka, has Ham been on the block?"

"I don't know, Smooth."

"You know someone set me up, and I only fucked with you three when I was down here. Banga was already dead on Sunday when I talked to Ham, and he was asking for help to post a million-dollar bond. When did you learn of Banga's death?" Smooth asked.

"Just like everyone else around here, I learned of it the same night he was killed. You had to be asleep not to know that he was killed," she informed Smooth.

"Damn it, Meka! I was good to yo' cousin! Ham set me up, Meka!" Smooth said, frustrated.

"Don't worry, baby! Cousin or not, snitching is against all rules and codes. I won't let him sink you," she promised.

Smooth looked at her with a new respect, and smiled. "I know you won't, boo!" Smooth said.

3

SMOOTH COULDN'T BELIEVE it took him two months just to sniff out the rat. Ham was so close to him that to consider either him or Meka as the rat would be an insult. But now he saw it clearly. After seeing Meka, Smooth returned to the dorm where other federal inmates were housed pending their trials. Smooth's cellmate was a Jamaican man in his forties named Rosco, who was indicted for tax fraud. He was the only person Smooth associated with and allowed in his cell other than Rosco's cousin, who everyone called Baby Dread, who was the same age as Smooth. Baby Dread was deaf and also facing tax fraud charges. Smooth lay on his top bunk, still not believing Ham's betrayal.

Shit! He was ready to betray his own cousin! Smooth thought.

Rosco and Baby Dread were on the bottom bunk playing repetitive rounds of chess.

"Checkmate!" Rosco said while signing to Baby Dread.

"Damn it!" Baby Dread cursed, failing to defeat Rosco again.

"Smooth, you sure you don't want none of this, mon?"

"Nah, I'm straight. I'm really not feeling it today."

"I can tell. Whatever it is, it got you bed sick since you came back from visitation," Rosco acknowledged.

"The wrong bitch done come up here, and China won't be able to see me. So, what do I tell her when she comes and can't see her baby daddy? But, too, I found out who the rat is, so the visit was worth it."

"Well, son. That's exactly what you tell China. I'm sure she'll understand you, man," Rosco suggested.

"Being real is better than being sorry later, mon!"

"True! True!" Smooth agreed.

"Now, I'ma ask you this again. I'm tired of beating up on my little cousin, mon!" Rosco said.

"Okay, one game," Smooth obliged as he jumped from the top bunk and sat down in Baby Dread's spot.

Smooth set up the black chess pieces while Rosco set up his. When Rosco was done, Smooth waited patiently while Rosco contemplated his first move. Rosco pushed his pawn in front of his queen two squares up.

Smooth did the same move and locked up their first pawns.

"Smooth, son, you listen to me carefully. No one knows you, mon, like you know your army. This rat must go 'fore you can defeat these federal armies," Rosco said as he pushed his second pawn two squares up next to his locked pawn.

Without time to reflect, Smooth followed suit and locked pawns again. Rosco's next move came fast and bold when he pulled out his queen in front of his pawn lined up with Smooth's king.

"I know. I've been thinking all day how the fuck I can checkmate this nigga without giving my next move away," Smooth spoke in code of killing Ham before he made the next bold move of standing off his queen with Rosco's queen.

"Mmmm! You're a bold lion, huh?" Rosco said.

"I've been losing and watching too long not to be bold," Smooth admitted.

"It's time for you to take chances with the army you've built, Smooth. Your team must come together to set you free," Rosco informed.

"These wires are too risky, old man."

"Yeah, but there's risk in every step you take, mon. It's 'bout being careful, young'un!" Rosco said as he sacrificed his queen by eating Smooth's queen. "Now we have ourselves a game where a pawn becomes the significant piece—just like your still loyal men out there," he continued.

Sue Rabbit, Guru, Spencer, and China, Smooth thought.

Three moves later, Rosco checkmated Smooth with his bishops, making it impossible for Smooth to move out of check.

"Damn it! How the fuck you always winning?"

"Because, mon. I got tired of losing," Rosco stated as he gestured for Baby Dread to sit back down.

"I'ma go jump on the jack," Smooth said.

"Be careful, mon. They're always listening," Rosco warned.

"I will. Thanks," Smooth replied as he strutted out to the phone to call China.

China picked up the phone and then quickly accessed the prompts.

"Hey, baby. You must be wondering where I'm at." China's voice clearly spilled through the line.

"Nah, baby. I was just calling to tell you to go ahead and see Jenny."

"What the hell you talking about? I'm in Martin County now. It's only 2:00 p.m.," China said, turning down the volume to Rihanna's "You Needed Me."

Here it goes! Smooth thought.

"Listen, baby. Some shit came up. I'd rather we discuss it when you come back."

"Are you okay, Smooth? Did you get into a fight?" China asked with concern.

"Nah, baby. It's nothing like that. I'm okay."

"Nigga, you done dropped the soap, and somebody done tore you a new asshole, huh?" China joked.

"Watch yo' mouth, China. I'll die before I let a nigga try me in this shit!" Smooth defended himself, despite knowing that she was only kidding around.

"Well, I'm at the Hess gas station down the street. I guess I'll get back on I-95 and continue north."

"Tell—"

"You have sixty seconds left," the automated voice said.

"Tell Jenny I said hello, and you drive safe, okay! I love you, China."

"I love you too, Daddy."

"Thank you for using GTL," the automated voice said before disconnecting the call.

Now I gotta tell Amanda not to show up here this week, because China's coming, Smooth thought as he dialed her number and got a persistent ring and then voice mail.

Damn! Where the hell is she? he thought as he dialed her number again, only to get the same results.

"I'll call her after lockdown is over," Smooth said out loud as he walked back to his cell to prepare for his rematch with Rosco.

He had only beaten Rosco in chess twice before, and he believed deep down that Rosco let him win those two games.

The man is a beast in this shit. The right man to have on my team too, Smooth thought as he watched Baby Dread get checked and then checkmated in the next two moves.

Damn! Smooth thought.

* * *

15

Ham was alone at home while Tina was at her doctor's appointment. Since being released, he had smoked all of his stash and was now fiending for some more crack to put into his lungs. He was paranoid to go out into the world, because he was ashamed of himself for turning state against Smooth.

With only $30,000 put up to supply his habit, Ham had no one to go to who would give him the crack he needed. Smooth was in jail, Banga was dead, and he was afraid to ask the niggas suspected of Banga's death. He was too paranoid to approach anyone.

They'll kill me like they killed Banga! Ham thought as he banged his crack pipe on the table to loosen the residue.

He gathered the residue, put flame to it, and then deeply inhaled.

"Yesss!" Ham exhaled, letting the crack smoke crawl from his mouth and nostrils. "The last of a dime breed," Ham stated, speaking of the last form of crack he had just smoked.

* * *

"Come on, Stone. You're really gonna sit here and play this thuggish game with me? All your fucking workers are giving you up, including the man you're trying to protect," DEA agent Jones said to Stone, who was sitting at the interrogation table for the sixth time in two months.

He was being held in the federal unit without bail until he gave up the man everyone had been calling Smooth. More than 35 percent of Smooth's operation had given the DEA his street name. No one knew his government name, and the DEA and FBI were scratching their heads trying to pull him up in their data files, but to no avail.

"Mon, you continue to ask me 'bout a mon me never heard of," Stone said.

"Bullshit! Even your men tell us he's your fucking connect!" Jones exploded, slamming her fist down on the metal table.

Behind a mirror-tinted glass, her boss and partner were watching closely. They knew she was a pit bull in a skirt and would soon have Stone Bolt singing like Usher, the more she pulled him from the cell and brought him over for questioning.

"Look! You could make this shit light on yourself, Stone," Jones suggested, standing up and gathering the photos she had of the man everyone called Smooth, "or you could take the long bus to a federal joint for a long-ass time. I hate putting my own people away for their ignorance."

"Bullshit, mon! You do it with fucking honor, bitch!" Stone screamed.

Agent Jones was tired of the name-calling every time she interviewed Stone. He made it his business to call her out on her name as a woman.

Agent Jones removed her can of pepper spray from her waist, shook it twice, and sprayed the entire can in his face.

"Ahhh! Shit, bitch!" Stone cried out, unable to defend himself since he was handcuffed to the table.

"Now I got your bitch!" Jones said before departing from the room with a shrilling Stone left behind.

When she entered the booth where her boss and partner were waiting for her, they were both laughing and enjoying the entertainment.

"I knew it was coming. The pit bull in a skirt finally got tired of the name-calling," Jones's boss laughed.

"I bet he'll be calling the devil a bitch in the next hour!" Agent Jones stated as she sat down and took a sip from her mug of cold coffee.

1

AMANDA WAS ON her sofa regretting missing Smooth's calls. She was in a deep sleep and had her iPhone on the charger on silent, so she never heard the calls. She was watching Steve Harvey on television while thinking of Smooth.

I can't wait until this shit is over with, she thought, when she heard knocks rapping on her door. *Who the hell is that?* she wanted to know, since she was not expecting any visitors.

She got up from the sofa and went to answer the door. When she looked through the peephole, she saw that it was Smooth's homeboy, who Smooth had brought over once before. Amanda sucked her teeth, unlocked the door, and then opened it up.

"May I help you?" Amanda spoke with an attitude.

"Hey, Amanda, do you remember me?" Sue Rabbit asked.

"Yes, I remember you. Now what is it that you want?"

Damn! This bitch already trippin'! he thought.

"Listen, can I step inside to discuss something private with you?" Sue Rabbit suggested.

Amanda didn't trust anyone, but being that Smooth introduced them, she gave him the benefit of the doubt.

Smooth wouldn't bring anyone to my place who wasn't trustworthy, Amanda thought.

"Come in," Amanda said as she stepped aside to allow Sue to enter.

When Sue Rabbit entered, Amanda walked to the living room and turned off the television. The apartment was dead silent.

"What is it?" she asked.

"Amanda, can I take a seat?"

"Sure, but let's not get too comfortable," Amanda permitted.

Sue Rabbit sat down on the sofa, released a sigh, and then spoke. "Listen, Amanda, we're all uptight about Smooth being in jail, and we can't bond him out. If he had a bond, he would be home, and that's no question," Sue Rabbit explained to Amanda, who stood up and crossed her arms as she listened. "Smooth left a team out here, and as a team, we gotta hold him down."

"Smooth is straight," Amanda said.

"We know he's straight, Amanda. And while he's gone, I want to do what I got to do to make sure he is straight."

"And how will you do that?" she asked.

"By making sure his turf is protected, Amanda."

"Oh my gosh! Is you people crazy? The DEA just did a big sweep, and you guys still want to play with them?" Amanda asked.

"Amanda, we don't see the DEA, and the DEA don't see us. We were never targets, Amanda."

Sue Rabbit stopped short when Amanda's phone chimed in blasting Rihanna's ringtone. When she saw that it was Smooth calling, she held up her index finger directing Sue to hold on momentarily.

After getting by all the automated prompts, the call connected.

"Hey, baby. Sorry I missed your call."

"It's okay. How are you?" Smooth asked.

"I'm okay. I'm having a chat with one of your boys who just stopped by."

"Who is that?" Smooth asked curiously.

"The only one you brought over," Amanda replied, looking over at Sue Rabbit.

Smooth knew that she was talking about his second-in-command. And he knew the only reason Sue Rabbit would be at Amanda's was to cook up some product.

"Is he on business?" Smooth asked.

"I'm suspecting. We haven't got that far," Amanda began.

"Listen, that's my boy, baby. Whatever he needs, handle it for him, okay?"

"Yes, daddy," Amanda said without protest.

"Let me holla at him," Smooth ordered.

Amanda looked at Sue Rabbit, who was all ears, and handed him her iPhone. "He wants to speak with you."

Sue Rabbit grabbed the phone and spoke. "What's good, homie?"

"Shit! You tell me, bro?" Smooth shot back.

"I just thought that it was time for me and Guru to shake the dust from our shoes and get shit back popping. We out here to hold you down, bro," Sue Rabbit informed him.

"I appreciate everything y'all two doing, man. I know that the other part of the equation is going to be hard to solve without China. So give me time to see what I can do for the team," Smooth told him in code language, indicating hooking up Sue Rabbit with his connect.

"That'll be nice, soldier. Real nice," Sue Rabbit said.

"You boys have to be careful, like really careful. We're all walking on eggshells. When China gets back, I need you to meet with her and get all the information she'll have for you."

"You have sixty seconds left," the automated voice said.

"Okay, bro. I'll do that. Here's Amanda before the phone hangs up," Sue said as he hurriedly handed the phone back over to her.

"Hello."

"I love you, baby. Make sure he gets taken care of."

"Okay. I love you too."

"Thank you for using GTL," the voice said as the call was disconnected.

When Smooth was gone, Amanda looked at Sue Rabbit.

"How much is it you need cooked up?"

"That's what I'm talking about!" Sue was exhilarated.

"Boy, all that's not even called for! Now how many we need to cook up? And know that it's $1,000 for every five," Amanda informed him.

20

"I need fifty of them done tonight," Sue said.

"Well bring them over to the other apartment. The same rules apply. No more cooking at my spot," Amanda said.

"I got you. Thanks."

"Don't thank me. Thank Smooth. Because without his word, I wouldn't be doing shit!" Amanda told Sue Rabbit.

"I respect that, Amanda."

* * *

China lay in her bed at the hotel and thought about what Smooth had to tell her. She would only be able to see Jenny for one day, and she was resting until it was time to drive over to the prison. Then she would be back on the road traveling south to go visit Smooth. Like with all of her visits with him, she was eager to see him.

She rubbed her stomach after eating a pint of butter pecan ice cream and a handful of chocolate cookies. The baby kept her munching, and it seemed that she gained weight every day.

I can't believe I'm about to be a mommy, she thought while looking at the small knot in her stomach.

She was almost three months pregnant, but she could still hide her pregnancy if she wanted. But she was too excited to hide her gift from anyone. China recalled when she had first learned of her baby. The Arab doctor had emphasized the positive in the most beautiful way China could ever imagine. After her morning sickness and the incapability of keeping down her food, Roxy and GaGa advised her to take a pregnancy test. She wasn't fond of Walmart's quick tests, so she went to visit the doctor for possible STDs. Instead, her results came back that she was pregnant.

Amazing! China thought as she closed her eyes and dozed off to sleep in no time.

* * *

When Javier pulled up to Roxy's soul food restaurant, he pulled in next to a blue Suburban and rolled down his window. The window of the Suburban rolled down at the same time.

"What the news over here, esé?" Javier asked his M-13 brother, Marco, who was keeping an eye out for China to show up at the restaurant.

"Like always since we've been coming here. The bitch hasn't shown her face. It's like she knows we're watching. Or maybe it's her watching us, homes," Marco said, passing a kush blunt to his M-13 brother named Jr. sitting in the passenger seat.

"I'm sure she'll show up soon. If not, we just gotta make her come to us, homes. Her sister owns the joint," Javier informed Marco.

"That'll be a piece of cake, esé."

"I know. Let's just give her a couple more days before we act on that suggestion, amigo," Javier continued.

"Okay, homie. Just know, we watching this spot with an eagle eye," Marco said.

"Good, because that's what we're gonna need, Marco. So let's continue to keep our eyes open," Javier said as he backed out of the parking space and departed.

"I can't wait to meet China," Marco told Jr.

"Me neither. I want to see how sideways Chinese pussy really is," Jr. replied with an evil smirk on his face.

5

"JENNY DAVIS. REPORT to visitation," the CO announced over the PA system.

"There you go, baby," Carlisha said to Jenny, who was lying down on her bunk cuddling with her.

"Yeah, that's China," Jenny said as she stripped out of her gym shorts and grabbed her visitation uniform.

Jenny wore nothing but her white cotton Hanes panties and a gray sports bra, which turned on Carlisha.

Damn, I have a bad-ass bitch! Carlisha acknowledged as Jenny applied cocoa butter lotion to her flawless, brown lustrous skin.

"Let me lotion your legs for you, baby."

"Okay," Jenny said as she turned around and squirted lotion into Carlisha's palms. She then turned back around and let her apply the lotion to her back and inner thighs, all the way down to her ankles.

Jenny loved the delicate touch of Carlisha caressing her body.

"I could never get enough of loving your body, baby. If China don't know, she definitely has a prize in her life," Carlisha said.

"I think she knows that, boo," Jenny said, looking back at Carlisha with her hands clamped on her hips.

"Damn! I wish we had time. I'll eat that pussy before you go. What's up?"

"No, Carlisha, I have to get going," Jenny said, moving fast at putting on her nicely creased uniform.

She knew the look in Carlisha's eyes meant trouble, and before Carlisha could force her into a quickie, she was getting herself out of the cell. She appreciated Carlisha's superb sex game, but her number one bitch was waiting to see her. And everyone in the prison knew that China came before any bitch.

"I'll take you up on that offer when I come back, baby. See you later," Jenny said, blowing Carlisha a kiss before she hurried out of the cell.

When Jenny made it to the visitation room, she immediately spotted China sitting at the table with an assortment of food.

Damn! She's already picking up weight? Jenny noticed about her.

"Hey, baby!" Jenny said as she embraced China and gave her a passionate kiss before sitting down at the table.

"You're smelling good. What? Did you shower in cocoa butter before you came?"

"You know I had to get the next bitch off me. I can't come up here smelling like no cunt now," Jenny said.

"You are so wrong for that one," China laughed.

"It's the truth, boo!"

"I know. That's the funny part!" China said, still laughing.

"What's up with you? You're already gaining weight, baby," Jenny said.

"I know, and I'm only almost three months," China purred.

"Damn! I can only imagine what six months will look like," Jenny said, biting into a hot chicken sandwich.

"Yeah, I know."

"So, how is Smooth?"

"I go see him tomorrow. He has something to tell me that he couldn't tell me over the phone, and it's running me crazy of what it could be!" China explained.

"Well, stop always expecting the worst, baby. Shit! Maybe he's ready to sign them papers."

"No man will marry me from behind bars, Jenny. Sorry, but it will never happen," China said as she took a sip from her water bottle.

"You mean to tell me that you will not marry Smooth if he asks you to do it now?"

"Exactly what I've told you. Hell no! That's not my dream approach, and I will not settle for it!" China told her.

"I don't blame you, baby. A bad bitch like you deserves a king and queen wedding with horses, golden roads, and beautiful white doves flying off into the beautiful sunset," Jenny stated.

"Girl, you're so full of it!" China laughed.

"For real, baby! Just let me be there. Shit! I only have three more years as of today."

"Really? Shit! I thought it was a little more. That's good. I can't wait until you come home, Jenny."

"Me too, baby!"

* * *

The DEA couldn't hold everyone they had picked up in the sweep two months ago. So those who weren't facing major drug indictments were able to post bond and be back on the streets, trying to hustle lawyer money to keep them free and put up money to keep them straight in case they had to do a bid in prison for their charges.

The beef between the M-13s and Smooth's soldiers was still breaking out. Money had spotted the Lincoln Town Car further down the block before it started creeping. He had put everyone on the block on beat. Money held an all-chrome AK-47, with his finger on the trigger.

"Yo, Sunny! Duck off! Let me squeeze on these dumbass Mexicans!" Money shouted to his homeboy, Sunny, who was also watching the car creep from the dark confines of an apartment complex.

"I got 'em in the—"

Chop! Chop! Chop! Chop!

Before Sunny could get the words out, he was hit by the assassin who no one saw standing up in the sunroof.

Money quickly acted and returned fire at the Town Car, which slammed on the gas, coming his way. SUVs came from every direction onto 110th, releasing a deadly fusillade killing anything moving.

"Damn it, man!" Money shouted, realizing that he was at odds.

Before he became a dead statistic, Money ran through a pathway that led him to the other street.

The Mexicans came with strategy, Money thought as he ran and ducked from the shots trying to take him down.

These Mexicans are not resting! Money reflected as he hid in some bushes.

He stayed there until the threat was gone and the sirens flared. He couldn't go back on 110th, or else he would be walking back onto a crime scene.

Damn it! I need Mall out here with me, and Choppa to come out of his coma, Money thought as he walked to a trap house on 109th and lay low until the heat died.

It didn't help that Mall was sitting in the county jail without bail. Mall was looking at some serious federal time and being ratted on by unknown workers as he sat.

Money was fortunate to dodge major indictments. He was able to bond out from the sweep with the help of his baby mama, Tabby, who constantly reminded him to put up money in case he was ever arrested. Now he was out hustling for a good lawyer and preparing to welcome his first child with Tabby.

I can't let these Mexicans kill me out here. I got too much to lose to die in these streets, Money thought as he sat on the sofa in the trap house.

He needed at least $50,000 real quick to put down on a lawyer who would promise him no time in prison. Then, whatever he gained after that would go to his seed and baby mama.

I definitely gotta get on my grind and stay alive, Money considered.

6

WHEN CHINA PULLED up to the Martin County Jail, it was just hitting 5:00 p.m., and she knew that was the time Smooth would be coming off lockdown.

"Perfect timing!" she said as she exited the Benz SUV and walked toward the jail.

Staring at the many small windows of the jail, China wondered which one was Smooth's cell and if he could see her walking up to reception. It was her third time visiting him since his incarceration, and these same thoughts would always run through her head.

Once inside, China approached the receptionist and waited patiently for the receptionist to attend to her. It took every bit of five minutes, and China felt disrespected standing and waiting for the receptionist to come take her name.

These bitches about to make me stunt up in this bitch! China thought, with a mean look on her face.

"Sorry, ma'am, may I help you?" the receptionist said over the microphone.

"Yes, I'm here to visit inmate Donavan Johnson," China said with an attitude.

"Give me a moment, please," the receptionist said as she looked in her computer for Smooth's location.

China stood a long minute before the receptionist came back on the mic.

"Ma'am, booth 27. He will be there shortly."

"Thanks!" China replied as she rolled her eyes at the heavy-set black woman and strutted away to the visiting lobby.

These muthafuckas would make me get Miami on them in this bitch! China thought as she found booth 27, sat down, and waited for Smooth to show.

When Smooth came through the door and saw China waiting for him, he knew beyond any doubt that his baby was indeed pregnant. It was evident from her weight gain. Her cheeks were getting chubby, and her nose was getting fat, he noticed.

"Damn, baby! You could have told me that I was looking for a new China. You're already picking up weight," Smooth said to her with a smile on his face when he picked up the phone.

"And yo ass must be stressing or you're getting your food taken, because you're losing weight!" China said as she took notice of his decreasing weight, that he wasn't aware of himself.

"Never that! I'm eating like a hog, and I'll kill a nigga trying to take anything from me," Smooth said.

"I know you would. So how are you, and has the lawyer come to see you yet?"

"Nah, that useless muthafucka ain't come see me in two weeks as of today."

"Well, we'll just get you another lawyer. One from Miami this time. I don't trust these people up here," China said.

"That'll be nice. Last time I did see him, he wanted me to plea out to twenty-five years, telling me I had no hope for trial," Smooth informed her.

"Smooth, twenty-five years? What is he thinking, and why are you just telling me this shit?"

"Because, China, I don't need you stressing. It's not good for the baby," Smooth replied.

"You being gone twenty-five years out of our life is supposed to feel better, Smooth?" she asked as tears fell from her eyes like a stream.

"Baby, I'm not getting twenty-five years. That was only the first offer, which will go down with the right mouthpiece," Smooth said, making her calm down.

"Baby, are you preparing to do time?" China asked as she wiped her eyes.

"Baby, I don't know how this shit will play out. I was set up, and the only good thing is I know who set me up!" Smooth announced, giving China an impish smile as she caught onto his intentions.

"Oh really?" China replied, with a smile on her face.

"Without him, there's no case, huh?"

"At least half of it, baby," Smooth admitted.

Smooth was still stuck with possession of the one hundred kilos the feds found in the Range Rover stash spot. But with the snitch incapable of testifying, Smooth could shake the probable cause and make the state attorney yield a sweet deal or drop the case.

"Is he local?" China asked.

Smooth nodded his head up and down.

"Yeah, so listen to me careful, China. I need you to locate Rebecca's brother and have him come see me so I can deal with this nigga," Smooth told her.

China was ready to do anything to help Smooth come home to his family.

"Where the hell do I find him? Does Sue Rabbit know?"

"No! They never met, something I intentionally did," Smooth said.

"Smart, I guess," China stated.

"Something like that! But to find him, look up Eric Spencer. He's an ex-militant."

"I know, baby. I got the name. So, I guess this is some good damn news, baby," China smiled.

"Yeah, I want to talk to you about something else, China."

"Why does it sound like it's not my cup of tea now?" she said.

"It may not be, baby. But I need you. Sue Rabbit is my second-in-command, baby."

"And?" China said, with sarcasm in her voice.

"Please hear me out, China. Damn! Let's not turn this visit into a damn battlefield," Smooth said while China held a pout on her face.

"What is it, Smooth?"

"Like I was saying, Sue Rabbit is my second-in-command. I need you to make a trip and get double quantity."

Is this nigga out of his mind? China thought, realizing that Smooth was asking her to venture into the dope game.

"Smooth, do you realize that we're about to be a family, or is you just saying fuck that?" China asked with an attitude.

I knew this shit wasn't going to be easy, Smooth thought, biting down on his teeth and trying to bridle his anger. "China, all I'm asking is you to help me out. A nigga got niggas that…"

"Smooth, it's all about your niggas. Don't you know that's what separated us the first time?" she exploded.

"China, what separated us is your damn stubbornness. I've worked hard to build what I have in them streets. I can't leave my niggas starving because I'm incarcerated. All I'm asking is for you to carry my load, baby, and watch my back. China, come on!"

"Smooth, I have your back like nobody else. Don't even go there with me!" China said sternly.

"Then continue to have my back. If you don't want to do it, pay for a driver, baby."

"You're still asking me to do something I just don't want any part of, Smooth! You're not getting the picture!" she explained.

"So you're telling me to just say fuck Sue Rabbit, huh?"

"Them are your words, Smooth, not mine!"

"But they're your actions, China! Who do you think had my back when you were in prison?" he asked.

"Smooth, you damn near got killed. Where was he at then, huh?"

"Woman! You're so damn stubborn!"

"Fuck you, Smooth! The only stubborn muthafucka I see is you! Why won't you just leave that shit alone?"

"I will when I make it home, China. I promise," Smooth told her sincerely.

Smooth was serious, and China knew him too well to doubt him. When he said something, then he was a man of his word.

"Are you sure, Smooth?" she asked.

"Yes, baby. I'm sure. But until I get there, I'm still in charge of the streets, China, despite your unwillingness to take any part in it. We stepped in this shit together, and I'm not throwing no dirt in your face. I'm just saying I need you to help me continue to stack this paper. I'm giving you my word, China, that when I jump, I'm out of the game. And it's just gonna be about us, baby—our family. Just please help me out until I can get there and hand everything over to Sue Rabbit," Smooth begged.

China looked at Smooth and saw in his eyes that he was serious.

He's making a promise to me, China thought. *With Smooth operating from jail, at least I don't have to worry about losing him to a bullet by one of his enemies.*

"You come home and you're done, Smooth!" China said, staring him in his eyes.

"Done!" Smooth agreed.

"Let me sleep on this, Smooth. I'll make up my mind and see if I'm gonna do it or not."

"That's fair!" Smooth said, bridling his excitement.

He knew that if China had to sleep on a decision, her mind was already made. What he didn't know was that he was putting her and their child in danger.

* * *

Stone sat in his cell and couldn't believe how his workers were giving him up along with Smooth. Stone knew Smooth's real name well, unlike his workers who he had listened to on a tape just hours before in an integration room giving up Smooth's street name like it was nothing.

I can't believe these soft-ass niggas just turned state on me! Stone thought angrily while pacing in his cell.

It was midnight, and his cellmate was asleep. His bodyguards and two lieutenants were sure to pay for their infidelity. He had looked out for all of them equally and fairly.

I gave them niggas anything they asked for. For them to cross me at the end, mon! he reflected.

He needed to get out, but he had no bail and a lengthy federal indictment. In spite of all the restraints, Stone still had connections to make all his betrayers pay for their disloyalty.

I just need to get in contact with my man, to handle business without these muthafuckas listening to me conversation, mon, Stone thought as he stood at the cell's door and stared out into the wing.

He could hear a couple toilets flushing every few minutes, which indicated that he wasn't the only one up thinking of a way out of federal housing unit 9, where everyone was looking at thirty to life on major federal charges.

I gotta get in contact with my boy and let him know that the streets are setting him up, mon, Stone thought to inform Smooth without tipping the feds off to his location and identity.

* * *

"Damn, baby, this dick is good!" Roxy purred as Sue Rabbit pounded her hard from the back.

Roxy's face was buried in her silk pillow, and she had pulled all the sheets off their king-sized bed.

"Yes, daddy! Beat this pussy!" Roxy demanded while throwing her pussy back into Sue Rabbit's deep penetration.

She was using her pussy muscles at the same time, blowing Sue Rabbit's mind; he loved the tricks her pussy could do. It was the best pussy he had since being in Miami, and the pussy that made him leave his sideline bitches alone. Sue Rabbit surprised himself at how he fast he fell for Roxy. There was no doubt that he had found a queen among queens.

She had her head on her shoulders and wanted Sue Rabbit to fall back from the dope game. She was about to open two more Roxy's soul food restaurants between North Miami and the keys. Business was sprouting, and she needed help from her man on how to manage it.

"Oh shit, baby! I'm coming!" Roxy shouted as she came to a mind-blowing orgasm.

"Arrrgghhh, shit!" Sue Rabbit groaned, exploding his seed deep inside of Roxy's pussy, matching her orgasm.

Roxy squeezed Sue Rabbit's dick with her pussy muscles until he was done sending all his seed up her tunnel. He then collapsed onto the bed all sweaty and panting.

"So you're tired now, huh?" Roxy asked as she climbed on top of him and lay on his chest.

"Tired isn't the word, baby. Because I'll never get tired of making love to you," Sue said breathlessly.

"Me either, baby. I can't get tired of you, baby," Roxy replied as she leaned over and softly kissed Sue Rabbit on his lips.

"Baby, I need to ask you something, and I need your honest advice too."

"What is it, baby?"

"Okay," Roxy started as she sat up, straddled Sue Rabbit, and then looked deep into his eyes. "I'm about to open up two more restaurants, but after I pay for them to be built, it will be all the money I've saved up to make this happen. Am I making a smart decision by using up all my savings to invest in two more restaurants? Or do I need to save up some backup money? The thing is, I feel that if I don't do it, then I'm leaving open an opportunity for someone new to take over, baby, and I don't want that!" Roxy explained.

"Listen, baby," Sue Rabbit began, moving Roxy's hair out of her face. She threw back her head and slung her hair onto her back. "Baby, when your mind tells you to plan, you plan. And when your heart tells you to execute, then you execute, baby. You've been saving your money to invest since the moment you planned on opening up two more restaurants.

Now you have it, baby. So all you have to do is trust in your investment, the same way you trusted in saving up for your investment. Now will be a wonderful time to expand your business. But are you ready to step up your game? That's the ultimate question to ask yourself," Sue told Roxy, who smiled because she always loved the way Sue wouldn't sugarcoat anything for her.

"Yes, baby. I'm ready," Roxy replied.

"Then I will be there with you every step of the way, baby," Sue Rabbit promised.

"Thank you, baby," Roxy said, being touched by his words.

"Baby, I have something else that I want to talk about," Roxy added.

"What is it?"

"Are you planning to retire from the game and come help me manage the restaurants? It'd be nice to have you over at least one of them," Roxy suggested.

"Leaving the game alone is in my plans, and sooner than you think, Roxy. Just give me a little more time, and I promise you that I'm retiring from the game."

"So you're really thinking about letting it go, huh?"

"It can't last forever. And we fall short by believing that it does," Sue Rabbit told her.

"I wish Smooth could have seen it like you, baby. Now he's caught in a sticky situation, and there ain't no telling when he'll be home," Roxy said.

"He'll be home. Just got to find him a good-ass lawyer. Me and Guru are trying our best!" Sue Rabbit informed Roxy.

"Is there any way I can help? Smooth helped me start up this business. There's gotta be something I can do," Roxy said.

"That's sweet of you, baby, but Smooth is being well taken care of. When you get a chance, just write him a letter and express your gratitude," Sue Rabbit suggested.

"Okay, baby. I will do that."

"And instead of two restaurants, we're gonna open up four of them!" Sue Rabbit exclaimed.

"But I only have money for two at the moment," Roxy reminded him.

"Well, now you have enough for four of them at my expense. And by the time I do retire, we'll have Roxy's soul food restaurants all throughout South Florida," Sue stated. "Daddy is here for the long ride and will be happy to help you make your dream a reality."

Roxy was at a loss for words. But she now understood what her mother GaGa meant when she said that God brings people into each other's life for a reason.

Sue Rabbit is definitely my soul mate and the man who God has sent into my life to help me, Roxy thought as tears fell from her eyes—tears of joy and real happiness.

"I love you, Trayvon," Roxy said.

"I love you too, Roxy. Trust me! We will see it through," Sue Rabbit promised her as he guided his again-erect dick inside of Roxy's wet pussy and made love to her once again, until dawn came upon them, and then Roxy had to get ready for work.

7

TINA COULDN'T BELIEVE that she was due to have her baby boy in two months. Ham was just as excited as she was, and was staying home with her every night. They were living off the $30,000 that Ham had saved up, but they were burning through it fast. When Tina fell asleep, Ham would sneak out through the night and drive over to another hood called Golden Gate in Martin County in his used, illegal box Chevy Caprice. He paid $800 for the badly conditioned Chevy so that he and Tina could get around. In Golden Gate on Bonita Street, Ham would meet with his crack connect and buy an eight ball of crack cocaine. Tina had started to pick up on Ham's habit now that he was always around. But she was too frightened to confront him and sometimes paranoid that he would notice her addiction.

Ham had just left the apartment, and, like always, Tina had crawled from the bed to her hidden stash spot in the bathroom. While sitting on the toilet, she put flame to her crack pipe and took a long, deep hit. When she heard the knocking at the front door, she damn near shit herself. She quickly fumbled with the pipe, jammed it back into the pouch, and tossed it under the sink.

Who the hell is that? Tina said to herself as she sprayed the bathroom with air freshener.

Satisfied, she walked out of the bathroom, down the hall, and to the front door.

When she opened it, she saw that it was Meka, Ham's cousin, who never came by.

"Hi, Meka. Ham's not here," Tina said with smoke breath.

Meka wasn't naive. She knew the distinctive smell of crack smoke on a fiend's breath. The first thing she did was look down at Tina's huge belly. *Damn!* Meka thought. "Well, where the hell is he at while you're in there smoking that shit? Does he know you're smoking again, Tina?" Meka asked, with an evil look on her face.

"What the hell are you talking about?" Tina defended herself.

"Bitch, don't play with me!"

Smack!

Meka exploded and then slapped the shit out of Tina, who stumbled backward and almost tripped over Ham's boots.

"Bitch, does my cousin know you're smoking again?"

With tears cascading down her face, Tina sat down on the sofa and hugged her stomach.

"No, Meka. He doesn't know. If he did—"

"He will kill you, Tina. You're harming your child. Don't you care?" Meka questioned.

"I know!" Tina shrilled. "I need help, Meka!"

"Don't worry, Tina. I will help you if you let me. I can't stand to see you mess up an innocent child's life. I was a crack baby myself, and they took me from my mama. You're almost due, Tina. You don't want that to happen to you," Meka explained as she hugged and consoled her. "Promise me you'll quit now, and I won't tell Ham shit. But you got to stop putting the baby at risk, Tina!"

"I promise, Meka. I will stop."

"Go bring me the crack and the pipe," Meka ordered.

"Okay," Tina said as she strutted off to the bathroom to retrieve the pouch in which she stored her crack pipe and crack.

Meka couldn't believe that Tina was so nonchalant toward her baby's health. She had come to probe Ham about his sudden release. Before she finalized her consideration of conspiring to kill her own cousin, she had to make sure that the facts were correct and that he, in fact, had set up her sex friend. When Tina returned with the black pouch, she handed it over to Meka.

"How long have you been doing this?" Meka said.

"A month after. Maybe two. I'm not sure."

"A month or two after what?" Meka asked Tina to be specific.

"After I found out that I was pregnant," Tina replied.

"So, there's a 90 percent chance that this baby is highly affected by these drugs?"

"I can't help it, Meka. I need help!" Tina pouted.

"Don't worry. Like I said, I got you. Now where is Ham at?" Meka inquired.

"I don't know. He stepped out and probably won't be back until later on tonight."

"Is he on foot?"

"No! Ham has a car now. He bought a Chevy for $800 when he got out of jail," Tina explained.

"Tina, who the hell bonded Ham out on a million-dollar bail?"

"I don't know the circumstances, but he wasn't bonded out. The state dropped the charges."

"But wasn't he caught with two ounces?" Meka asked.

"Yeah."

"Damn! He's a lucky bitch. No wonder he laying low."

"He said he don't trust the streets. And since Banga's gone, niggas have started acting different. Ham believes that someone from where he hustled at set up Banga and will try to do the same to him. So, he stopped hustling until his baby comes," Tina explained as she sat back down on the sofa.

Meka sat down on the ruined love seat and listened to her.

She has no clue that her man is the damn police, Meka thought.

Meka opened the pouch and dumped the contents onto her lap. "You gotta leave this shit alone, Tina. You're too damn young to be strung out on crack. And you're about to be a young mother," Meka informed her. "That's not easy, and you have to be a strong bitch!"

"I know, Meka. I promise I will stop."

"When Ham comes home, I want you to call me, okay?"

"Okay. I have to get your number. Wait a minute; don't Ham, have it?"

"I don't want Ham knowing I'm coming over, or his ass will try to run from me too," Meka said.

"Is he in some trouble?" Tina asked.

"Nah, just a little family trouble. He owes me some money, and I need my shit. You don't want him to know about this," Meka said, holding up the crack pipe, "then make sure you call me when his ass in bed asleep," Meka demanded.

"Okay. I will call you." Tina shook her head.

"Good," Meka replied as she exchanged numbers with Tina.

* * *

Spencer pulled up to Roxy's very crowded restaurant in his silver Camaro Z/28. He sat for a moment and observed his surroundings. Seeing no threat, he pulled out his iPhone and dialed China's numbers. She picked up on the second ring.

"Hello."

"I'm here sitting in the parking lot. Where are you at?"

"I see you. Come to the car with the flashing headlights," China directed.

When Spencer looked around, searching the parking lot for the flashing lights, he immediately spotted the Benz SUV.

"I see you," he said as he hung up the phone.

Spencer then stepped out of his Camaro and strutted over to China's Benz. When he hopped into the passenger's side, he sighed and then spoke. "Good to see you, China. We finally meet."

"Yeah, you do look like your sister."

"No, she looks like me! I'm the big brother, and she was the little sister," Spencer corrected.

China was happy to see Spencer in person finally, after drudgingly searching for him on the Internet. He had a Facebook page without a profile picture, and there were so many Spencers. It took her weeks, but now she had found him.

"So, what's up with Smooth?" Spencer asked, keeping his eyes on the parking lot and any movement.

He noticed that China was doing the same thing, unaware that she was moving with the same precaution as him.

"He's doing alright. He wants to see you," China replied. "He knows who set him up, and he needs you to work your magic. But I want to be there when you snatch him up."

"I don't know about that. I operate alone," Spencer responded.

"Well let me be frank, Spencer," China began as she turned in her seat and stared Spencer straight in his loud blue eyes.

China knew a killer when she saw one, and it was becoming evident to Spencer that he was staring back at a killer himself.

"You can snatch him up, but I will have Smooth order you to not kill him. I want to kill him. I'm making your job light by killing the man who has my man sitting in a cell," China expressed.

"If Smooth tells me to not kill him and to let you do it, then I will not lay a hand on this target," Spencer said.

China smiled and then offered her hand for Spencer to shake. "Thank you, Spencer," she said as he shook her hand.

Spencer was liking everything about China. He could tell that she was a straight killer and female to have on his team. *Damn! Smooth's a luck man!* Spencer thought. "Where do I go to see Smooth?" he asked.

"We'll go see him together this weekend," China said. "By the way, nice car," China complimented Spencer on his hot Camaro.

"You like it, huh?"

"I just said nice car," she replied, causing Spencer to break out into laughter.

"You're funny, China. I see why my sister loved you," Spencer said.

"I loved her too, and I miss her a lot!" China replied sadly.

"Just know she's in a better place and always looking down on us," Spencer added.

"I know."

China and Spencer sat in the car for an hour getting acquainted with each other. They clicked well and had a lot of common ground. But China kicked Spencer out when she felt an attraction coming along.

"Okay, I'll meet you here Friday afternoon. You have my number if any change of plans comes up on your end," China said to him as she started the engine.

"Okay. Ummm, I'll call you Thursday night," Spencer said as he stepped out of the Benz and strutted over to his Camaro.

"Damn! He's handsome and favors Rebecca a lot," China said as she drove away in her Benz. "I wish he was a woman right about now. I would put it on his ass," China said as she accelerated through the light.

* * *

"That's a bad-ass Benz, esé!" Marco said to Jr., who was twisting up another kush blunt.

When Jr. looked up and saw the Benz merge into traffic, he agreed that it was a bad one.

"That's a Mercedes-Benz ML350," Jr. said, knowing his cars better than anyone Marco had ever known.

Neither of them had any idea that they were staring at their target: China. She had come up from behind them, and neither of them ever noticed her.

"That Camaro is a bad-ass one too," Jr. said, pointing at the silver Camaro leaving the restaurant lot.

"Esé, it's been two damn months and no sign of this bitch. I say we make our move on her sister tomorrow and see if we can lure her this way," Jr. said, putting flame to the blunt and exhaling a cloud of smoke.

"I'll bring that by Javier and see what he wants to do. I feel like a waiting duck every day we come to this shit!" Marco admitted.

"We'll never be a sitting duck, homie," Jr. said, passing the blunt. "I think she's laying low waiting for daddy to come home."

"That nigga is dead, esé. I hear he got popped with a hundred bricks in the wrong town. That's the word on the streets," Marco stated. "And from up top, the DEA has no clue who he is. All they know is Smooth, and they don't even know that Smooth is in a federal holding cell in Martin County."

"Damn, esé! I won't be surprised if these street informers lace them up about him," Jr. said.

"Yeah."

"That's why we have to catch this bitch. If he does come back, he'll come back to the bitch's bones!" Jr. stated.

"You just want to fuck the bitch before you kill her, huh?" Marco asked Jr.

"Exactly!" Jr. said with an impish smile.

* * *

"Mmmm! Shit, daddy. Fuck me harder!" Jane ordered her new friend and victim named David.

David had met Jane at Roxy's and got her number just hours ago. She made it clear to him that she was only interested in a good fuck. When David attempted to put on a condom before having sex with Jane, she lured him with her superb oral sex to forget all about it. He had no chance to retrieve the condom when she threw him on the bed and climbed on top of him and then slid down on his erect dick. For an hour straight, the twenty-two-year-old had been fucking the shit out of Jane without a condom.

"Mmm! Yes, daddy! Fuck me harder!" Jane purred loudly in ecstasy as David pounded her pussy from the back with long, powerful strokes.

David had no clue that his one-night stand was a full-blown AIDS patient who had it out to kill every young man who gave her attention. Her new medication had her looking like a swimsuit model with a nice lustrous ass and lips.

"I'm coming, daddy!" she shouted as she came to her orgasm.

"Arrgghh, shit baby!" David released inside of Jane, who immediately pulled away from him.

"Boy, I don't need no damn more kids!"

When David looked down at his dick and realized that he had on no condom, he cursed himself for slipping up. "Sorry, baby!"

"It's okay. This pussy will always be the bomb. You don't need to worry. Just next time wear a condom," Jane told him with a smirk on her face. *Got him!* she thought.

8

MONEY HAD JUST pulled up to the red light when he looked over at the Hess gas station and saw the two M-13s walking inside. For a month, he had been getting the shit end of the stick, but he now had a chance to return the favor.

"Come on, light!" Money said impatiently as he grabbed his ski mask and Glock .22 from underneath the driver's seat. On his lap set his twin fully loaded Glock with hollow points.

As the light turned green, Money smashed on the pedal and quickly turned off into the Hess station and circled one time before he parked out of the camera's view. He slid the ski mask over his face and waited for the two Mexicans to come out of the store. His luck turned bad for him when a Miami-Dade Metro Police cruiser pulled up to purchase gas.

"Fuck!" Money exclaimed, hitting the steering wheel.

The police officer slowly walked into the station at the same time the two Mexicans stepped outside. Money decided to take his chances while the officer was inside. He opened the door, with Glocks in both hands, and stepped out. The Mexicans walking back to their lowrider Explorer never saw Money.

Boom! Boom! Boom! Boom!

When the police officer heard the shots erupt from outside, he instinctively grabbed his Glock .21 from his holster and ordered everyone in the gas station to get down for their safety.

"Get down everyone! Metro-Dade Police!" He then called for backup as he ran out the door to pursue the suspect running back to his car: "Shots fired at the 2100 East Hess gas station. All units respond."

"Freeze! Drop your—"

Boom! Boom! Boom! Boom!

Before the officer could get the words out, he was shot repeatedly in the face.

Money hopped in his Mercury and burnt tires, leaving the scene before any other police pulled up. When backup did arrive, they found their fellow officer dead.

"Officer down and unresponsive," an officer yelled into his radio.

* * *

When Smooth walked into the visitation room and saw Amanda at booth 30, he smiled and was delighted to see her. There was something about Amanda, though, that he couldn't put his hands on at first sight. *Something different!* Smooth thought. "Hey, baby girl."

"You make me feel like a little girl when you say that," Amanda said. "How are you?"

"I'm doing good now that I'm seeing you," Smooth answered. "How are you? Are you okay?"

"Boy, stop! You know I'm okay."

She's losing weight, Smooth thought, finally realizing what was different. "Baby, are you stressing?"

"Every day that goes by and you're sitting in this hell hole, Smooth, I'm stressing," Amanda explained.

"Baby, I'ma be alright. And I need you to be strong for me."

"I try, Smooth. But it's not easy not having yo' ass around," she admitted.

"It's the same with me."

"Shit! You've lost weight yourself. So don't jump down my throat, mister!" Amanda said, acknowledging Smooth's weight loss.

"I don't understand. I eat goulash every night with Rosco."

"Who's Rosco?"

"My cellmate. He's cool people. The Jamaican I wrote you about, remember?"

"Oh yeah, I remember. He's the only person you associate with," Amanda replied.

"Stand up and let me see that ass!" Smooth ordered Amanda.

She dropped the phone and stood up to model for Smooth. She put her hands on both hips and smiled seductively at him.

"Turn around!" Amanda read Smooth's lips.

She turned around, and Smooth definitely saw that she was losing weight. Her lustrous ass was slimming down, when it was once phat like a round juicy peach. Despite what he discovered, he still liked what he saw. Amanda was a beautiful woman who no man could walk past without checking out, regardless of how much weight she lost.

"Satisfied?" she asked when she sat back down.

"Yes, I am. I gotta kick Rosco out of the cell when I go back."

"For what? So you can jack that dick for me?" Amanda asked.

"Hell yeah!" Smooth replied, biting down on his bottom lip like Amanda loved to see him do.

"If it wasn't for these cameras back here, I'd show you how hard you got this dick right now!" Smooth said, badly wanting to stand up and show Amanda his erect cock.

"Don't worry, baby. You'll be home to feel the walls of this tight pussy," Amanda said to cheer him up. "I miss you,

Smooth."

"I miss you too, baby," Smooth replied.

Damn! I need to tell her! Smooth thought about informing Amanda that he and China were expecting a child.

Amanda knew that he and China were back on good terms. He had told her that if China ever caused him to leave her, there would be no reunion. He would go to Amanda and give her what she wanted—to be number one. Smooth tried his best to muster up the courage to inform Amanda, but he couldn't. He didn't know what reaction she'd have, and he was scared that he would lose her, which was something he didn't want to do.

After visiting with Amanda, Smooth went back to the dorm and hopped right on the phone and called China, with whom he couldn't get in contact.

Damn! Where the fuck is she? he thought as he tried her one more time, but again to no avail. He was expecting to see her with Spencer the upcoming weekend. *She's probably asleep catching up on rest*, Smooth thought as he then walked to his cell.

The cell was empty when Smooth looked around for Rosco and Baby Dread. He found them in front of the TV attentively watching an NFL game between the Cowboys and Saints. His mind went back to Amanda. He pulled his sheet off his bed and set up some privacy. Smooth then sat on the toilet, closed his eyes in retrospection of Amanda, and masturbated.

* * *

China stepped out of the shower and sauntered into the bedroom. When she grabbed her phone and saw the missed call from Smooth, she cursed herself. "Damn it! I was waiting on my baby to call!" she exclaimed as she sat down on the bed and continued to dry herself off with her Polo towel.

Zorro lay on the end of the bed and stared at her. She giggled when she imagined what Zorro was probably thinking in his head while looking at her nudity. *He probably lusting his ass off!* China thought.

She walked to her dresser and dug into her panty drawer. She found a pair of silk panties and slid them on, and she then looked for a bra. When she looked at the clock on her nightstand, she saw that it was about 10:00 p.m. She was expecting Spencer to call her all day. It was Thursday, and tomorrow she would be driving down to Martin County to go visit Smooth. Afterward, she would part ways with Spencer and go see Jenny and then Jefe.

My entire weekend is booked and busy! China thought as she pulled back her coverlet and climbed into bed.

She was tempted to call Spencer just in case he had forgotten to reach her, but she thought it was his responsibility and not hers.

Shit! He knows what tomorrow is! Besides, he made the offer to call on Thursday, not me! she thought as she closed her eyes.

It seemed like she was only asleep for a minute when her iPhone chimed with Rihanna's ringtone. She looked at the clock and saw that it was 11:58 p.m.

"Who the hell is this?" China wanted to know as she stared at an unlisted number, which she then answered out of curiosity. "Hello?"

"China, it's Spencer. Umm, I'll be ready tomorrow. What time?" Spencer's voice spilled through her phone and into her ears.

"Spencer, you find a good time to call me. I've been waiting on your call all day," China said.

"Sorry! But some things came up, and I had to handle business. But I did stick to my word. It's still Thursday!"

"Yeah, and its Friday in the next minute, Mr. Funny Guy!" China said, trying to sound serious. "But I do accept the apology."

"Thanks. I'll see you tomorrow. What time?" he asked.

"At 6:00 a.m. Jump behind me when you see me," she said.

"Okay, China. See you in six hours," Spencer said before he hung up.

China almost didn't want Spencer to go, but she couldn't explain why. There was just something about him that she liked.

Maybe it's because he's a killer like me, China thought.

When she reached over and put her phone back on the nightstand, she felt moisture between her legs. She reached her hand inside her panties and felt wetness. She was horny, and it all stirred up from hearing Spencer's elegant voice.

No! What the hell am I thinking? Smooth would fucking kill me if he knew his homeboy hit man just got my pussy wet! China thought, feeling like she was betraying Smooth.

"There is no way I would ever give Smooth's pussy away!" China said to herself before she closed her eyes.

China awoke to her iPhone waking her out of a deep sleep. She immediately noticed dawn peeking through the drapes, and that told her that it was past 6:00 a.m. Dawn came at 7:45 a.m.

"Fuck!" China cursed out loud as she answered the phone. "Hello?"

"Someone's late! I've been waiting over an hour!"

"Well, I told you 6:00 a.m., and I know it can't be no later than 7:45 a.m. That's not an hour of waiting on me," China said as she looked at her clock on the nightstand. "Oh shit! Sorry, Spencer. I'm coming."

"That sounds more like it!" Spencer said before hanging up.

It was 8:00 a.m. and China still had to drop off Zorro at Miranda's. It was a good thing she had packed her things the day before and everything was in her Benz. China threw on some pajamas and then grabbed her keys and phone and Zorro's leash.

"Come, Zorro!" China said to the dog, who came running up to her and allowed her to snap on his leash.

China flew downstairs, set the house alarm, and made a dash out to her Benz.

* * *

When Spencer saw China pull up next to him, he rolled down his window and then looked at his G-Shock watch.

"It's 9:45. Almost another day. I was on time, and you are late!" Spencer said and then whistled loudly. "Gotta be more on time!"

"Shut up, Spencer! While we're here, I'm going to grab us some breakfast. I'll make it up to you, so wait for me just a little longer," China said as she rolled her passenger window back up.

China grabbed her Prada purse and stepped out. She then walked up to Spencer's driver-side window that was still down.

"Anything you don't eat that I need to know about, white boy?" she asked.

"I'll eat a human alive. What on earth wouldn't I eat?" Spencer answered.

"Is that supposed to gross me out? The funny thing is that I believe you!" China said as she strutted off toward the restaurant.

Spencer looked at China's ass jiggle at every step she took, and instantly became hard.

Damn, Smooth! You're a lucky muthafucka! he thought while watching her ass bounce.

The smell of Roxy's breakfast had China hungry, while the sight of China had Spencer hungry.

* * *

"Yo, esé! That's the bitch China. She's walking into the restaurant," Jr. exclaimed, waking up Marco.

Jr. turned around in his seat to look at the cars parked behind him to see what car she had pulled up in. The Benz was the only car that had just pulled up to the restaurant, and it was parked next to the silver Camaro.

"Man! Let's get this bitch!" Jr. said, double-checking his Glock 9 mm while Marco called Javier.

"Hola!" Javier answered.

"Man, guess who just pulled up for breakfast, homes?" Marco said to Javier, who had just stepped out of the house.

"Hillary Clinton, esé?" Javier replied, speaking of China.

"Yep, and she's looking real good too."

"Okay, snatch her. Don't kill her. Mario wants to do it himself," Javier said.

"Is that all? So, are we permitted to fuck her, boss?" Marco asked Javier.

Javier wouldn't mind getting a chance to fuck China himself. He smiled when his dick got hard just thinking about fucking her.

"Yeah, esé. Fuck her, and save room for me!" Javier answered.

* * *

"So you're going to see Smooth like that? Did you look in a mirror before you left?"

"Shut up, Roxy! Smooth will not get to see me like this," China told her sister.

"Hi, China!" Tabby spoke up as she and Jane came out from the back to give her a hug.

"Damn, girl! You sure know how to get ghost on a bitch and act brand new!" Tabby said, with a protruding belly from her pregnancy.

"Yeah, and don't even know a bitch 'til it's time to collect rent," Jane added.

"Bitch! I have to get it just like y'all getting it. My man is the landlord, let's not forget!" China said as she hugged Jane.

"And you're getting thick too. You sure you're not pregnant?" China asked.

"Bitch! Don't wish that shit on me. I already have too many as it is!" Jane said. "That comes from eating this good-ass food here!"

"I'll agree to that. Now, ladies, get back to work. China, your food is ready," Roxy said. "Don't even try it, China!" Roxy said, stopping China from trying to pay for the two separate meals she had ordered.

"Roxy!"

"No, China. I will not accept it. I already charged it to my bill," Roxy told her.

"Thank you, Roxy. I love you," China said as she grabbed the two separate bags of food.

"He gotta get his own drink. I'm not carrying all that shit!" China said.

"Who is he?" Roxy asked.

"Damn, bitch! Touch your nose!"

"Smooth's going to kill you giving his pregnant pussy away!" Roxy said.

"For your information, I'm not giving no one any pussy. Dick is not on my mind, and the right bitch is not in sight," China corrected Roxy. "Plus, he Smooth's homeboy. How would that look?"

"Like something that happens every day in American," Roxy answered. "Drive safe and tell Smooth I said hello."

"I will!" China said as she waved goodbye to Tabby and Jane.

"See you girls later. Maybe we can go out when I come back in town," China told them.

"Okay, drive safe!" Tabby and Jane said in unison.

"I will!" China said as she walked toward the exit of the restaurant.

China stepped outside with both hands occupied. She was holding the food in two separate bags stacked in one hand while she held her orange juice with the other and had her purse hanging from her arm. "I really have to get on the road. I'll be able to catch the night visit after five o'clock."

China stopped short when a black Suburban pulled in front of her with a Mexican aiming his Glock 9 mm at her, a blue bandana wrapped around his face.

"Bitch! Get in the car before I blow your damn brains—"

Before Jr. could get the words out, China dropped her food and ran as fast as she could while digging inside her purse for her Glock .45.

"Get her!" Marco shouted to Jr., who was already out of the Suburban and on China's heels.

"Spencer!" China screamed as she ran toward his car. She was halfway when she felt a hand grab a handful of her locks and knock her to the ground. She lost control of her Glock when she hit the ground.

"Bitch! Where you going?" Jr. shouted as he punched her in the face with the butt of his gun, causing her nose to instantly start to bleed.

He then punched her in her stomach with all his might. He stood up and kicked her as hard as he could in her stomach. China was too hurt to holler in pain, and she had no wind left in her body. Marco pulled up and hopped out to help Jr. toss China into the backseat. When Marco bent down to pick her up, China heard shots fired and then felt the warm blood from Jr.'s head splatter onto her face. His body fell on top of her. She heard more shots exchanged and saw the second Mexican shooting himself out of an ambush. China was in serious pain, and all she could do was lie down and wish that she died faster. The second Mexican managed to escape.

When China opened her bloody eyes, she saw Spencer pulling the dead Mexican, who had beaten her and her baby, off of her.

"China, I'm here!"

Spencer's voice was the last thing China heard before she immediately passed out and saw nothing but darkness.

9

MARCO WAS FURIOUS—as was Mario, who was throwing a fit. It was everywhere on the news: Attempted abduction gone bad. One suspect was dead while another was on the loose. It was on every radio station as well.

Police were everywhere looking for Marco, whose description was being accurately displayed everywhere.

"How the fuck did y'all miss her partner?" Mario asked Marco, who was sitting on his sofa drinking his fifth Budweiser.

Marco didn't want to tell Mario that his eyes were closed when China pulled up, and Jr. was no longer alive to bring it up.

"I . . . we never seen him pull up, esé!" Marco stated.

"But y'all saw her pull up?" Mario asked as he came and stood in front of a very nervous Marco.

Mario smelled something, but he just couldn't put his hands on it.

"Man, esé! We fucked up!"

"Of course you fucked up, esé! Now we have a delay in getting this bitch. I'm sure her security will be airtight now," Mario said as he walked over to his bar and poured himself a shot of Mexican rum.

Javier sat on another sofa and was just as furious as the others. He was looking forward to fucking the shit out of China before Mario killed her. Now he had to wait until she slipped up again.

"Mario, I will go after her myself," Javier offered.

"I can't, Javier. You're no longer infantry. You're a leader. And leaders send out their troops to handle war, and their troops are supposed to do what, Marco?" Mario asked.

"Their troops are supposed to bring the leader progress and victory," Marco replied.

It was one of the rules of being an M-13 gang member, and Marco knew it well. It was the reason that many other M-13 members died, just like Jr., who was unable to bring victory to his leader. Marco realized how lucky he was to be alive. He had survived the gunfight against the white man. Now he had to survive the war against Smooth's retaliation.

"Mario, I'm a bring you victory. Just give me time to let the block calm down," Marco swore.

"In two weeks, I want you to get back out there, and keep your eyes on the prize," Mario ordered. "Do we understand each other?"

"Yes, esé!" Marco replied.

* * *

When China came around, she found herself in a hospital bed hooked up to an IV machine. Her head was pounding, and she felt like it was about to explode. When she tried to get up, a hand landed on her chest to prevent her from moving. When she looked to her side, she saw Spencer and felt immediately comfortable.

"Doctors don't want you moving too much. By the way, welcome back," Spencer said, with a smile on his face.

"How long—" China cleared her throat to clear up her scratchy voice "—how long was I out?" she finished.

"Today would make the same day, China. But you proved to be a soldier. You lost a lot of blood."

"How? Was I shot?" she asked.

"No. I did all the shooting."

"Oh my gosh!" China exclaimed while feeling her now flat stomach.

The little knot was no longer there, and it didn't take China long to realize that her baby was gone. China began to shake badly as the realization continued to dawn on her that her baby was gone.

Spencer had no idea how to put a bandage on someone's hurt as China broke down, so he simply grabbed her hand and squeezed it. "I don't know your pain, China, but I can assure you that I will not sleep until I catch Mario," he said.

China was touched by his words of support. She looked up at Spencer and threw her arms around his neck.

"Thank you so much, Spencer!" China sobbed into his strong arms.

Spencer felt someone else's presence in the room, from behind. He turned around and saw the nurse walk in with her clipboard in her hands.

"Sorry to interrupt. I'm Tara, and I'm back to check your vitals," the nurse said.

"She's fine to me," Spencer replied, causing a chuckle to arise between the nurse and China.

"Awww shit!" China winced in pain after smiling too wide, which irritated the stitches on the bridge of her nose and upper lip.

"I was just about to inform you of your condition," the nurse said as she read from the clipboard. "You went through three operations successfully after removing the remains of your fetus from your womb. Thanks to your friend, you were rushed to our Jackson Memorial Hospital by an ambulance, which arrived and immediately took precautions with your miscarriage. You were losing a lot of blood, but you made it to us on time. The stitches you just felt on your face were to close up some deep gashes, which will take two weeks to heal," the nurse explained.

"Your sister stopped by, but she had to run back to the restaurant. She told me to call her when you woke up," Spencer said, staring directly into China's eyes.

"Let me check your blood pressure real quick, and go get you some pain medication if you don't mind," the nurse said as she squeezed herself between Spencer to begin checking China's blood pressure.

While Tara took her vitals, Spencer called Roxy.

"Perfect again. It's 110 over 70. It's like nothing ever happened to you," the nurse said as she documented China's vitals on her clipboard. "Now I know it may be a little difficult to eat, but is there anything you want from the kitchen?"

"Ice. My throat is on fire!" China said.

"Okay, I'll order it right away," the nurse said as she left the room.

"Your sister and mom are on their way back up. I wish I could stay, but I can't."

"You don't have to run from my family," China said, cutting him off. "You saved my life, and that scores big points in my book. Thanks, Spencer, for being there. Without you, I probably would have lost my life."

"They were trying to abduct you and bring you back to Mario," Spencer informed her.

"They killed my child. In two weeks, I'll be happy to meet Mario myself. Oh, by the way, we're still going to see Smooth."

"We can do that once you're healed," Spencer suggested.

"Listen, Spencer. A couple stitches and my baby kicked out of me will not keep me down. I have a man to help get back on these streets. No time to grieve. Plus, I have a new personal enemy to meet. And until I find him, I'ma be a busy bitch!" she informed him.

"Okay, Ms. Preston, here's your ice," Tara the nurse said, walking in with a tray of ice and beverages.

"I thought you'd probably want something cold to drink as well. Water? Soda? Juice? What's your pick?" she asked, pointing at each one individually.

"When will I be able to leave?" China asked as she selected a cold Pepsi and a cup of ice.

"The doctor prefers discharge no later than Sunday morning. So you're looking at a day of bed rest," the nurse informed China.

"That's perfect. Spencer, we'll be leaving Sunday morning. Is my car still at the restaurant?"

"Yes, next to mine. I rode over in the ambulance with you," Spencer replied.

"What time is it?"

"Almost 9:00 p.m.," Spencer answered.

Damn! I've been out cold since this morning! she thought.

"Get some rest. I'll be back on Sunday," Spencer said as he spun around on his heels.

"Spencer!" China called out before he made it to the doorway.

"What's up?" he said, after turning around.

Damn! I don't want him to leave, but why? she thought. "Thank you again," she said.

"You're welcome. I couldn't let them hurt you."

"Why?" China asked.

"Because! You're Smooth's girl," he said as he winked at her and then stormed out of the room, leaving China speechless.

Yeah. I'm Smooth's girl! China thought.

* * *

"These Mexicans are getting too bold, my niggas!" Sue Rabbit said to more than a dozen of his ranked lieutenants and sergeants in their new meeting location. It was a new trap house on 56th that only the people who were present knew of. Sue Rabbit and Guru didn't need Smooth's words to begin his retaliation. China was the queen of their operation and the sister of Sue Rabbit's queen in his life. Sue Rabbit pressed his comrades to spill Mexican blood on their turf. Sue looked over at Guru and nodded his head. Guru walked from behind the minibar and handed him a dro blunt.

"We gonna hit up the Mexican joint on 127th and leave everything flatlined." Guru gestured with his hands.

The room exploded into ovation, ready to spill blood for China.

"She is one of us, and we will not allow these Mexicans to get away with bringing harm to her. She was pregnant and lost her soldier—" Guru paused and gave the room a look over to search his lieutenants' and sergeants' faces "—so we take away many of their soldiers tonight!" Guru ordered, followed by the room exploding into another exhilarating ovation.

"She's the queen bee!" Guru shouted.

"China! China! China!" the crowd began chanting.

* * *

After seeing the feed of Smooth's men gathered together and planning to retaliate in her name, China had a new respect for Sue Rabbit and Guru. The entire meeting had been recorded by Sue Rabbit and forwarded to Roxy's iPhone 7.

China was amazed and deeply touched by their support.

"Now I see why Smooth's so adamant about not leaving his homeboys by themselves. They are too loyal," China reflected.

"So, what do you think?" Roxy asked.

"I think Sue Rabbit and Guru are some real muthafuckas, Roxy!" China commented.

"The both of them were upset when they learned what had happened," Roxy explained.

"All of Miami knows, huh?" China asked.

"It's all over the news, China. Police are still at my damn restaurant," Roxy said.

"And you're sure Mom's going to be alright?" China asked Roxy, concerned about GaGa's recent high blood pressure attack from too much worry over her daughter.

"She'll be fine. She'll be here tomorrow to see you. She just needs some rest," Roxy assured her.

"Smooth's gonna flip out, especially when he finds out the baby is gone!" China said sadly.

"Hey! You're alive! Smooth will be grateful for that!" Roxy reminded China, which cheered her up a little bit.

"Yeah, you're right," China said.

"Excuse me, but visitation hours are now over. If you plan on staying all night, it's fine. But if not, the doors to this unit will be locked," an attending nurse informed China and Roxy.

"Well, I'll see you tomorrow," Roxy said, looking at her new pink diamond embedded Rolex. "Sue will have a fit if he comes home and I'm not there."

"Damn! That nigga got big sis fucked up in the head," China said.

"Whatever!" Roxy said, blushing and rolling her eyes while gathering up her purse to leave. "He's just a man who you can't leave home alone, and I gotta be home when he comes home."

"Yeah, I guess."

"Goodnight. Now get you some rest. See you tomorrow," Roxy said as she kissed China on her forehead. "Love you."

"Love you too, Roxy!" China said.

When Roxy was gone, China adjusted her bed and turned up the volume on a breaking news report in Miami:

"All day has been a steady disaster in the streets of Miami, of murder, attempted murder, and abductions, possibly stemming from this morning's attempted abduction of China Preston. We've learned that she is in stable condition, but sadly, she's suffered a miscarriage. Our latest breaking news is of the chilling murder scene on 127th here in Miami, where a Mexican strip club owned by the late Juan José Jr. was attacked. Police are trying to see if this is in retaliation for or in connection with the case of China Preston, whose abductors were members of a Mexican gang."

China changed the channel, with a smile on her face.

Sue Rabbit and Guru said they were going to attack 127th, and they did, China realized. "Now I see why Smooth cares so much for his men," she said quietly.

China's thoughts abruptly went back to the events of that morning and Spencer saving her life. She could still feel the kicks to her stomach that knocked the wind out of her, making it impossible for her to shrill in pain. But she could still feel the comfort that overtook her when she felt the blood of her attacker splatter onto her face. And she could still feel how safe she felt when she saw Spencer standing over her. China felt that she owed Spencer her life for backing her up. There was something more than the resemblance of his sister that China liked about him.

He isn't an ordinary white boy, China thought. *He's sweet, humble, and handsome.*

She then thought about her enemies, who were Smooth's enemies.

She was too caught up on seeking retaliation in her mind to notice the evil look on her face. By all means, she was ready to make Mario pay for what he had done to her life. She was very eager to become a mother, and now she was childless. *I will make sure I make Mario pay, even in hell, when I send him there,* China thought. She then closed her eyes, trying her best to prevent her tears from falling.

* * *

The Mexican man tied to the chair at the slaughter pad shook badly and was afraid of Spencer, who stood in front of him with a gasoline can.

"Tic! Here! Give our man a nice shower, will you!" Spencer said to Tic as he handed him the can.

"Hell yeah!" Tic said as he began pouring the gasoline all over the man.

"Mario, amigo!" Spencer said and then whistled. "Where is he?"

"No English, amigo!" the man said quietly.

"So we're on this no English shit again, huh?" Spencer said as he walked up to the fearful Mexican who was in his mid-forties.

Around the man's neck was a blue bandana soaked in gasoline as well.

"So you want to lie to me, fucker?" Spencer shouted.

Smack!

Spencer backhanded the man, causing blood to trickle from his split lip.

"No English, no English!" the man cried out.

"Yeah, I know, fucker! No English!" Spencer shouted, and then pulled a pack of Newports from his pocket.

He pulled out two cigarettes and tossed one over to Tic, who was sitting atop the gasoline can.

"I think he believes that we are some stupid Americans, Tic. What do you think?" Spencer asked as he pulled out a Bic lighter and lit his cigarette.

"Please, amigo!"

"Awwww! Please is English, amigo. Come on, I know you have a good memory. What is it that your teacher taught you, huh?" Spencer asked as he tossed the lighter over to Tic.

Tic sparked flame to the cigarette and then tossed the lighter back to Spencer, who had an evil look on his face.

The Mexican wasn't naive. He knew the mischief that was forming in his two abductors' minds. At the moment, he hated Mario and his affiliation with the M-13 gang. Living up to the M-13 gang was all he had done for more than twenty years now. Dying by a bullet was more expected than being abducted and tortured.

Fuck you, Mario! the Mexican named Angel thought.

"My amigo, you're really going to sit here and die for a man who doesn't care about you at all, huh?" Spencer asked, circling Angel while smoking.

"No English, no comprende!" Angel shouted.

When Angel raised his voice, it stopped Spencer in his tracks. Spencer turned around and looked Angel in his fearful eyes.

"Who the fuck are you screaming at, wetback?" Spencer shouted back as he took another pull from his cigarette.

Tic got up, walked around, and stood next to Spencer.

"Tic, do you like fried Mexicans?"

"I love fried Mexicans!" Tic responded.

Spencer looked at Tic and thought about China. Images of Jr. beating her came as a flash to him.

"You're gonna wish you knew English," Spencer said as he flicked his burning cigarette onto Angel, instantly igniting him into a tremendous flame of fire.

"Marioooo!" Angel shrilled in pain as the fire burned him, covering him in angry flames.

"I knew he spoke it," Tic said as he then flicked his cigarette on a burning Angel, who was still shrilling.

"Call Johnson and Miller, and tell them to clean up this mess," Spencer ordered Tic as he walked away.

"Got you, boss," Tic replied as he watched Angel burn to his bones.

10

AMANDA WAS AWARE of what was going on with China, but she didn't know how to really feel about her other than envious. She hated China with a passion, but she would never tell Smooth even if he asked. China was an obstacle in her way and someone who had the heart of the man she loved and wanted in her life.

It was 9:00 a.m. on Sunday, and Smooth hadn't called her yet.

He usually calls around this time, Amanda thought.

She wasn't sure if Smooth heard on the news about China or not. But she was ready to give his ass the third degree for not informing her about China's pregnancy.

"I can't believe he tried hiding that shit from me!" she said as she poured herself a glass of 100 percent orange juice.

She was up early, and cooked herself a small breakfast of scrambled eggs, cheesy grits, bacon, and ham. It was a single serving, and she was having trouble eating with a peaceful mind. Every time she thought about Smooth hiding China's pregnancy from her, she became disgusted. She hated liars with a passion, yet the man she loved had lied to her, even though he belonged to another woman.

Since he wanted to lie, I will make him pay for it, Amanda considered.

All she could think about was how Smooth had been about to leave her to be with his family. Now that was shut down, since China had lost the baby.

"I can't let him!" Amanda stopped short of speaking directly from her heart when her iPhone chimed on the table.

When she picked up the phone and checked the caller ID, she saw that it was Smooth. She answered and then listened to the automated prompts.

"This is a collect call from the Martin County Jail from an inmate named Smooth. To accept this call, please press zero. To refuse this call, please press the pound symbol," said the automated voice.

Amanda quickly pressed the pound button and then hung up the phone.

As badly as she wanted to hear his voice first thing in the morning, she just couldn't bring herself to listen to his lies and excuses. She wanted to make him sweat, and now was the best time to start it.

"I will make sure you will think twice before you try to lie to me again," Amanda said as she finished trying to eat her breakfast.

It was hard for her to keep Smooth off her mind, but she promised herself that she would try her best. Smooth called back twice, and neither time did she bother to answer the phone.

She finished her breakfast and then took a shower to get ready for her doctor's appointment. She had a yearly checkup at 10:30 a.m. She loved her doctor and wished that she could have her for a mother. Dr. Rosa Mendoza was a sweet and one-of-a-kind fifty-six-year-old Puerto Rican who looked nothing like her age. Looking at Dr. Rosa, most would guess she was in her mid-thirties.

Eating good and having the right man in bed was what Dr. Rosa always told Amanda was the secret to health.

Amanda was impressed with how well Dr. Rosa knew her patients' appointments in advance. Just last weekend, Amanda had bumped into her inside a Walmart and was reminded by the doctor to report for her appointment on time.

"That lady is like a god. She knows her children—all of them!" Amanda said as she took off her pajamas and looked at herself in the mirror. "Damn!" she said, realizing how much weight she had lost.

But how? When I eat and don't do shit. Lord! I'm stressing, she thought. *I can't let this man stress me out like this, especially when he's planning to leave me by myself in the future*, Amanda realized as she stepped into the steaming hot shower. *Damn it! I love him! And I fucking miss his ass!*

* * *

Smooth didn't know what to expect after hearing Amanda refuse his calls. His mind instantly went to the negative and the prospect of her sleeping with another man.

Is she sleeping with another nigga already? Smooth asked himself as he lay in his top bunk with a Silk White novel resting on his stomach. *If she is fucking with another cat, how could I be made?*

He was about to be a father and have his own family. Smooth loved China and couldn't see himself leaving her for anyone, not even Amanda, with whom he had grown closer over the years. Smooth was thinking of him and China and how things would be in life for them as a family.

He was a man of his word and would leave the game alone when he came out of his situation. He was writing down successful business plans to seek when he was a free man again. Miranda would waste no time helping him learn the ropes as a real estate agent. He still had property and would invest in more when he came home. Being incarcerated, Smooth was able to think clearly.

Despite hating his incarceration, he was grateful for a time-out. He wanted to leave there as a devoted family man, and in order to be successful, he had to discard the things that would hinder him from giving his best. The streets, money, power, and infidelity in his relationship with China had to go. *Sleeping with Amanda or any other woman has to stop!* Smooth realized as his mind instantly went to moments he had with Jane. *The world is grimy, just like her.*

She was China's friend who she had helped get on her feet fresh out of prison. And she had slept with China's man without any guilty conscience.

That's a cold bitch with some good-ass pussy! Smooth thought as his cock began to rise when images of him fucking her came to his mind.

In his mind, he went back to the first day he had sex with Jane. *She said she had plumbing problems, and I plunged her toilet until all the water was gone*, Smooth thought as he caressed his erection.

His cellmate was out to court, so he had the cell to himself for most of the morning. His thoughts of being faithful to China went out the window when he saw the sex face of Jane flash in his mind.

Fuck! Smooth thought in sexual frustration as he jumped down from his top bunk.

He snatched the sheets off his bunk and put up some privacy. He then sat naked on the chrome toilet and stroked his erect cock while thinking of Jane, whose pussy was one-of-a-kind and as much as he hated to admit it, better than China's.

I gotta reach out to Jane and tell her to send me some bikini pictures of that phat ass and pussy print, Smooth thought as he masturbated while thinking of her sweet, tight yet deadly pussy.

The last thing on his mind was why China hadn't stopped by the day before.

* * *

When China got wheeled through Jackson Memorial Hospital's doors, she was happy to see her hero standing there waiting on her with his passenger door open.

"Good morning, Spencer!" China said as the nurse halted the wheelchair in front of him.

"How are you, China?" he asked.

"I'd be better if I had me some breakfast."

"I picked you up some breakfast at your sister's restaurant. She fixed your favorite when I told her that it was for you," Spencer informed China as he helped her stand up from the wheelchair.

Damn! He smells good! China thought, smelling Spencer's Davidoff Cool Water cologne.

"You make me feel like an old lady, Spencer," China said, trying to downplay his affectionate affinities.

"Sorry!" he said as he closed her door.

China watched him utter a couple words to the nurse and then walk around and get inside the car. The luxury of Spencer's Camaro made her feel like she was home, a place she needed to get to so she could take a nice shower.

"So, where to first? Your car or home? I'm guessing home, huh?"

"How did you know?" China replied, with a smile on her face.

"Who wouldn't want to get home first," Spencer began as he reached into the backseat and grabbed China's breakfast and placed it on her lap, "to get a fresh shower and regroup."

"Thanks, Spencer."

"You're welcome, and you don't owe me anything."

"Thanks again then," China added while still smiling.

Damn! She's beautiful! Smooth, you lucky son of a bitch! Spencer thought as he pulled out and turned up the volume to his heavy metal by Seven Dust.

What the fuck is wrong with this crazy-ass white boy? China thought as she reached for the radio and turned the volume down to zero.

"Listen, crazy-ass white boy! This devilish-ass music isn't gonna cut it. How can you listen to that shit?" China asked Spencer, who was cracking up to the point of tears flooding his eyes. "That's not funny, Spencer!" China said, laughing herself.

Damn! He has a sexy-ass laugh too, she thought, instantly feeling guilty for adoring another man.

To hide her attraction, China bit into her ham and cheese breakfast sandwich.

"Sorry, China. But you're too damn funny!" Spencer said while drying his eyes.

When he looked in his rearview mirror, his entire demeanor changed from joy to being serious. China immediately sensed something was amiss.

"What's wrong?" she asked him, as a frown now appeared on his face while he still looked at his rearview mirror.

"We have some company. How about putting on your seatbelt," Spencer said calmly.

Without any hesitation, China did as she was advised.

"Two cars back is a Mexican who's been on my trail since I picked up my car. I thought I was tripping and that he was just another random guy, but evidently not," Spencer said as he slammed on his gas pedal while changing lanes.

The kickback from his powerful Camaro caused China's neck to jerk back.

"Damn! How about warning me next time, Spencer!" China shouted as he accelerated through traffic like a mad man.

When she looked in her side-view mirror, she saw the black Suburban trying to keep up with them. But the Camaro was too fast for the Suburban, and it was like a dog chasing a cat up a tree.

"What's your address?" Spencer asked.

"You're going the wrong way. We need to go east, Spencer."

"Before she knew it, Spencer artistically U-turned the Camaro and headed east, hopping onto I-95 and heading northeast. The Suburban was completely lost and didn't have enough horsepower to keep up. Spencer had lost them in less than two minutes.

"Where to now?" Spencer asked an impressed China.

"You've been watching too much *2 Fast 2 Furious*, Spencer," China joked before she gave him directions to her and Smooth's $2.3 million mansion, where no man other than Smooth had been with her.

After seeing how badly the Mexicans wanted her, China was ready to go door-to-door looking for Mario. "I gotta find this Mario!"

"No, *we* have to find Mario! Let's remember he just sent someone to kill me too," Spencer said. "And I don't know about you, but I don't take death threats lightly."

Spencer turned off an exit that would lead him to China's neighborhood.

"I can agree with you on that," China said as she took another bite of her sandwich with gusto.

As she was lost in her delicious sandwich, China realized that she didn't have her iPhone or her purse.

Damn! How the hell did I not notice it? she thought.

"Spencer, have you seen my purse—"

"And phone? They're in the backseat," Spencer cut her off.

When Spencer looked over at China, he saw her with another beautiful smile. Despite her swollen face, her beauty still shone through her injuries.

Damn it, Smooth! You're a lucky son of a bitch! he thought again as he pulled into China's enormous driveway.

Spencer reached into the backseat and grabbed China's Prada purse and passed it over to her. When China looked inside, she saw that her Glock .45 was still where she had last seen it. She was only a firm grip away from saving her own life. Then she remembered the Mexican man pulling her down by her hair, and losing her grip on her Glock.

"Don't worry, China. They'll never get that lucky again," Spencer said, after reading her mind from the discontented look on her face.

China looked up at Spencer and stared into his blue eyes.

"Thank you," China said, bridling her emotion. "Do you mind coming in? You can help yourself to whatever is in the kitchen."

"Sure," Spencer said as he exited the Camaro at the same time as China stepped out.

11

MARCO HAD LOST the fast Camaro and was pissed. Mario had suggested that he get back on China's trail in two weeks. But two weeks for him was just too long, and it would give China enough time to run and hide.

Marco had decided to drive back to the scene. There, he caught the white man who had saved China's life, and tried to kill him when he hopped into his Camaro. Now he was gone again, and Marco had no clue what direction the Camaro had gone.

"Fuck!" Marco exclaimed, hitting the steering wheel before he headed back to Miami.

* * *

For days now, Ham had not been well rested. Every time he did lie down, it was after he had made love to Tina and put her in an exhausted state. There were plenty of times when Tina could have called Meka to inform her that Ham was home asleep in bed. But she loved him too much to betray him. When she felt Ham easing out of bed, she rubbed the sleep from her eyes and asked him where he was going. "Where are you off to now?"

"Go back to sleep. I'll be back in the morning," Ham replied with a demanding tone of voice.

What the fuck is wrong with him, always stepping out if he's no longer hustling? Tina wanted to know as she sat up in bed, leaned against the headboard, and hugged a pillow.

Tina looked at Ham's silhouette in the darkness. She could see him digging in his pants before putting them on. Tina reached over and turned on the light on the nightstand to illuminate the room. Ham squinted from the bright light.

"Girl, cut that damn light off and go back to sleep!"

"No! Bring yo' ass back to bed, Ham. It's three o'clock in the morning. Where the fuck are you going?" Tina shouted.

"Listen, Tina. There's no need to get all worked up 'bout nothing."

"Ham, why are you leaving every other night and not coming back with shit?" Tina questioned.

Ham became upset and shot across the bedroom. He had his hands around Tina's throat in no time, choking her.

"Ham!" Tina squeezed out while clawing at his face and kicking wildly.

"Bitch! Why you questioning me, huh? I pay the muthafuckin' bills in this muthafucka. You hear me? Huh?" Ham screamed in rage as he continued to choke Tina until she passed out.

When he saw her body jerk and go stiff, he let go of her, afraid that he had killed her. But when he saw her chest rise and fall, he sighed a breath of relief.

"Baby, I'm sorry!" he apologized while backing away from her.

He felt terribly wrong for hurting his soon-to-be baby mother. Ham quickly put on his boots, grabbed his Glock .40 from underneath the mattress, and dashed out the front door.

* * *

Spencer and China were enjoying each other's company while driving back from New York in one of Smooth's stash cars. China had changed her plans of going to see Smooth on Sunday and instead drove to New York to see Jefe. She left Spencer at a hotel until she handled business with Jefe.

When China returned to the hotel room, she and Spencer laughed each other to sleep. When they got up and left that morning, they knew they'd be in Martin County to visit Smooth around noon. China found it odd that Smooth hadn't called her since she had been released from the hospital.

"I thought he at least would have called after we didn't stop by yesterday, Spencer," China said while driving south on I-95.

"How did you know I was up? You never looked over to see if my eyes were opened or closed," Spencer asked.

"Boy, we've been together twenty-four hours now. I think I know everything about you, except who the special lady in your life is."

"I don't have one. Too much stress. Plus, I stay on missions. A lot of missions," Spencer informed her.

"Poor excuse, Spencer!" China exclaimed.

"Why is that?"

"Because a man like you attracts a beehive of bees."

"I'm not all that now!"

Shit! You're a liar! China almost blurted out as she chuckled when she realized how close she was to really speaking her mind.

"What?" he asked curiously. "See, you even agree!"

"That is not why I'm laughing, Spencer. A thought just came to mind," she explained.

"What is it? Share it!" he said.

"Nope! It's my thought and your curiosity," China said, with a sexy pout on her face that made Spencer's dick jump.

Wow! I gotta get away from this woman, he thought. "I guess you got that one. Wake me up when we get there."

"What are you doing? Boy, it's time for you to take the wheel. There's no need to go to sleep," China stated.

Spencer looked at his watch and saw that it was his time to drive. They were splitting the eighteen hours of drive time, and China's nine hours were up in thirty minutes.

"Could we stop for some coffee?" Spencer asked.

"Sure!" China said as she pulled off an exit and shortly pulled into a 7-Eleven gas station in North Carolina.

"I'ma use the restroom while you gas up!" China said.

"Now you're giving me chores!" Spencer murmured.

"Not actually. I'm only telling you since you're driving the remainder of the way," China said as she strutted off inside.

"Damn, Smooth! You're a lucky son of a bitch!" Spencer said as he watched China sashay into the gas station in her skintight jeans and blouse.

After using the bathroom, China looked at herself in the mirror. The swelling in her face had gone down completely, but some redness could be seen on the bridge of her nose and upper lip. Despite the injuries, China was grateful to be alive. She knew that if it hadn't been for Spencer, she would have been a dead woman. China looked at her iPhone and double-checked for any missed calls. When she saw none, she became worried.

I hope he's not in any kind of trouble. Maybe he's in the damn hole! she thought. "I'll check with the jail at dawn," China said as she began to wash her hands.

When she was done in the bathroom, China grabbed some drinks and snacks for the rest of their drive. When she walked out of the gas station, Spencer was blowing off the steam from his cup of Maxwell House coffee that he drank straight black.

* * *

Ham felt bad about what he had done to Tina. She didn't deserve being hurt, despite what she had been through at such a young age. Ham didn't think about Tina's feelings, and like always, when he couldn't face the responsibilities of life, he ran away.

Ham drove thirty miles outside of Indiantown and Booker Park to Jupiter Island, which was a wealthy section of Martin County. Although it was a big risk, he had to make the trip or go for broke. Tina didn't know that the $30,000 was gone. Ham had smoked, gambled, and tricked with other crackheads around town.

On desperate days, Ham would travel around town and look for wealthy homes to burglarize. He had spotted a nice home in a real estate advertisement magazine. For two days and nights, he had watched the luxury home from his badly conditioned Chevy that stuck out like a sore thumb in the neighborhood. Fortunately, he was never seen by any of the residents.

When Ham pulled up to the residence he had be scouting, he pulled into the driveway and killed the engine and lights. He dug into the glove compartment and retrieved a pair of black leather gloves. As he slid them on, he closely watched the house for any signs of movement. When he saw none, he exited the car with a squeaky door and left it cracked for an emergency entrance just in case he had to make a run for it.

Damn, I wish I had a hit right now. I'd prefer to do this shit high as a kite, Ham thought as he crept around to the back of the house.

Ham walked through a wooden gate and entered the beautiful backyard, where a big swimming pool and guesthouse sat stagnant without any signs of life. Ham walked around to a side window to a room and tried to lift it up.

"Shit!" Ham whispered in a shout when the window didn't lift up.

He moved on to another window and got the same result. Ham became frustrated and very impatient when he realized that all the windows were locked.

Fuck this shit! Ham thought as he took his Glock .40 and smashed the den window to little pieces.

The loud shattering of glass was enough to wake the entire neighborhood. However, Ham was again fortunate not to raise any unwanted attention.

He entered the home through the den window and waited a moment to let his eyes adjust to the darkness. When he saw that he was alone, he moved to check for any occupants. He came to the first room and tried the door, only to find it unlocked. He stuck his head inside and found it empty. He knew that there were only four bedrooms in the home according to the real estate advertisement.

Ham then quickly checked the other rooms and found no one inside any of them as well. As he walked closer to the master bedroom, he could hear soft moans of sexual pleasure. He slowly tried the knob and eased open the door. A television was on mute, illuminating the room, and Ham could see the covers moving on the king-sized bed. It was evident that he had walked up on two elders getting their groove on. They were too caught up in their groove to notice the threat behind them.

"Oh, Bob, I love you!" the old woman purred as the old man pumped in and out of her pussy with long, powerful strokes.

"Patty, I love you, honey!" Bob replied breathlessly to his wife of thirty years.

"Oh, Bob! Fuck me harder!"

Boom! Boom!

"No! Bob!" Patty screamed when Bob's head exploded in blood and brains on her face.

"Bitch! Shut the fuck up!" Ham demanded as Patty jumped away from Bob and sat straight up against the headboard.

When she felt Ham staring at her naked breasts, she grabbed the covers and tried to cover her sagging tits and large erect nipples. Ham scared her when he snatched the covers away.

"I'ma ask you nicely, Patty, and one time only, or I'm going to fuck the shit out of your old ass!" Ham said as he pulled out his dick and showed Patty his enormous cock standing erect.

"Where is the money and everything worth something?" Ham demanded while stroking his cock.

"We have money in a safe in our home library. Please don't harm me. I won't report you," she begged.

Ham put his dick back inside his pants and then walked up to Patty. He roughly grabbed her by her red hair, yanked her head back, and then looked her in her bloody green eyes.

"Get me to that safe, woman, and I will let you live. If you try any dumb shit, you will die!"

Patty was trembling badly, to the point that you could hear her teeth rattling.

"I promise I won't try anything stupid," Patty pleaded.

"Lead the way, old woman!" Ham ordered her as he pulled Patty from the bed by her hair.

Patty walked naked with Ham to the library. Once inside, she pressed a button that accessed the safe, dividing the shelf on the wall. Behind the shelf, Ham saw the built-in wall safe. Patty entered in the seven-digit passcode and opened the safe. When Ham saw the neat stacks of money, he got excited and smacked Patty on her sagging butt cheeks. Patty jumped, out of fear, and moved to the side.

"Come here, bitch! We're 'bout to celebrate!" Ham said as he pulled out his erect dick.

"Please, mister, don't hurt me!"

"If I have to tell you again, I will kill you. Now turn around and bend over, old lady," Ham demanded.

As Patty did as she was told, Ham entered all of his cock into her from the back.

"Oh my Lord!" Patty shouted as Ham continued to plunge deeply inside of her pussy.

Ham fucked Patty like she was twenty years old. Her cries faded as she passed out unconscious from the unbearable pain to her senior vagina. As Ham fucked Patty, he stared at all the stacks of money and thought how lucky he was to pick the right home. He was back on the map and would make up with Tina for putting his hands on her.

After Ham came to his load, he shot his cum all over Patty's butt cheeks and then pushed her to the floor of the safe. He aimed his Glock at her unconscious body, shot her twice in the head, and then proceeded to clean out the safe. When he was done, he locked Patty in the safe and then left the scene unnoticed.

12

AMANDA TOSSED AND turned in her sleep all night until she gave up, got out of bed, and walked into the kitchen to fix herself a cup of coffee. She couldn't get the notion of Smooth lying to her out of her mind. It was Monday, and she had to stop at her doctor's office.

I'll go see him after I pick up my results and give him a piece of my mind, Amanda thought as she waited for her coffee to brew.

Despite Smooth's bullshit, she was missing him like crazy. She reminded herself about all the times they had sex, as well as the times when he simply held her all night. Although she was number two in his life, Smooth treated her like number one.

He has no clue how deep he's pulling himself in with me. It was only a matter of time before he left China and came to me, she thought. *But would he have left that bitch after finding out that she was carrying his child?*

She knew how baby mama attachments brought drama.

Was I ready to go through that with Smooth? she asked herself as she poured herself a cup of coffee and added cream and sugar to it.

"I can't let that bitch take my man. I've been playing the fool long enough. That nigga either gonna choose or lose," Amanda said as she took a sip.

She was definitely going to see Smooth today.

* * *

When Ham returned to the apartment, he was surprised to see Meka sitting on his worn-down sofa and hugging a crying Tina.

He was at a loss for words and high as a kite from smoking crack. After he had come up, he immediately drove to the Golden Gate area on Bonita Street and purchased five ounces of crack cocaine. Meka could see his decreased weight and the signs of a crackhead clearly.

This nigga smoking too! Meka thought as she continued to hold Tina in her arms.

"So you're a woman beater now, huh?" Meka said to Ham, who sucked his teeth and then stormed into the bedroom.

Meka hopped up from the sofa and went after him.

"Damn it! I'm your fucking cousin, Ham. Don't you ignore me! Nigga, you been acting crazy sense!"

"Them muthafuckas killed my cousin. These same niggas around this hood, Meka!" Ham shouted.

Meka could smell the crack smoke on him intensively. She couldn't believe how low Ham had become.

"Nigga! So you smoking? What else are you doing against the code?" Meka asked.

"Man, fuck you! Get outta my shit!" Ham exploded.

"Who the fuck are you talking to, Ham?" Meka asked, shocked that Ham was talking to her in a manner in which he had never spoken.

"You're high, nigga, and you need fucking help!" Meka exclaimed.

Ham tightened his jaws and looked at Meka, with his fist balled up like he was ready to pound her. Meka grew up fighting men her entire life, including some of Ham's battles. She stood eye to eye with Ham, fearless of his hostility.

"If you feel froggy, nigga, jump!"

Before Meka could finish, she sidestepped Ham when he charged her, and caught him with a quick reflex two-piece to his jaw. Ham stumbled and fell to the ground.

"Bitch!" Ham shouted as he came to his knees and tried to stand up. However, he went right back down when Meka kicked him in his face with her fur boots.

"I got yo' bitch, you snitching-ass nigga. You're hiding from your guilt, nigga. You set Smooth up!" Meka screamed at Ham before kicking him again in his face.

"Meka, no!" Tina cried out as she hopped on top of Ham to prevent Meka from kicking him again.

Ham was too high to defend himself.

"Yeah, bitch! I snitched on that nigga. So what! You want to kill me now? I thought we were blood. That nigga's not family!" Ham replied to Meka, after spitting a bloody tooth from his mouth.

"Nah, Ham! I ain't gonna kill you. It's not me you need to worry about," Meka warned him as she stormed out of the apartment before Ham could see how hurt she was.

Meka couldn't believe how bold Ham was. He had hate in his heart for Smooth. When she got into her Altima, she sat for a moment and wiped the tears from her eyes. She then pulled out her iPhone and replayed the entire conversation she had just had with Ham.

"Damn, Ham! Why? I love that man. You took something precious from me," Meka cried. *And then he has the nerve to be on crack, just like his baby mama!* she thought. "Don't worry, Smooth. Daddy coming home!" Meka said as she drove away from Ham's apartment.

She did what Smooth had requested of her. Now she would wait until he called her to give her further instructions.

When Meka pulled up to her apartment, she quickly stormed inside, locked the door behind her, and then stripped off her clothes. She hopped into a hot soothing shower and thought about Smooth. Meka rested her right leg on the edge of the tub and then began fondling her clit.

"Mmmm, Smooth!" Meka purred before she stuck two fingers inside her wet pussy flooding with her juices.

She thought in of how Smooth used to fuck her long, hard, and passionately.

He had been acting funny when his bitch came home. Now he will see how down I am for him, Meka thought as she intensified the strokes to her pussy.

"Uhhh, shit! Smooth!" Meka exclaimed in ecstasy as she came to an electrifying orgasm.

* * *

As China and Spencer walked toward the entrance of the jail, China was getting an incoming call from Smooth. "Fine time to call, don't you think?" China asked Spencer.

"Smooth?"

"Who else?" China said.

She ignored the call and walked into the reception area of the jail. China rolled her eyes when she saw the same receptionist sitting in her chair, scrolling down her computer with her mouse. To China's surprise, the receptionist assisted her as soon as she got to the counter.

"May I help you?" the receptionist said to China over the microphone.

"I'm here to see inmate Donavan Johnson."

"One moment," the receptionist requested as she looked up Smooth's name on the computer. "Booth 29. He'll be there shortly. Is he with you?" the receptionist asked, pointing at Spencer.

"Yes, he is!" China replied.

"Well, only one person back at a time. He will have to wait in the lobby until you're done," the receptionist informed China, smacking her bubblegum.

"Okay," China said as she walked away from the counter with Spencer.

As they walked to the waiting lobby, China turned around and caught Spencer checking out her ass in her skintight jeans. China pretended not to notice his gawking.

"I'll go back first and then let you kill the last fifteen minutes," China said.

"Okay. I guess I'll sit down and wait on you," Spencer said as he took a seat and pulled out his phone.

"Don't get yourself into any trouble," China joked as she walked off and entered the hall of booths.

He was staring at my ass. I saw him, China thought to herself with a smile on her face. *Men these days!*

When Smooth came into the room, sat down at the booth, and saw China's face, he almost lost his cool.

"Baby, what the fuck happen?" Smooth asked, enraged.

"Calm down, Smooth, and just be glad I'm alive. And definitely thank your friend Spencer for saving my life, baby."

"What do you mean? Did you get into a car wreck? Is the baby okay?" Smooth asked with concern.

It hurt China so badly to have to tell Smooth that she lost the baby at the hands of his enemies.

"No, Smooth. I didn't get in a car wreck." China paused, holding back the tears was impossible. "We lost the baby!" China said as the tears flooded down her face.

"China!" Smooth choked on his own tears, feeling a hole form in the center of his chest. "What happened?"

"Mario sent two of his men to snatch me up the morning I was coming to see you. Spencer stopped them. He killed one of them," China explained, catching her breath. "The other one got away."

"Fuck! I'm sorry, China," Smooth apologized.

"Don't be. I'll be okay."

"I'm putting Spencer around you like glue."

"No, Smooth. I can handle myself," China said.

"You have no right to say no. I want you safe," Smooth ordered angrily between locked jaws.

He was highly upset that he couldn't be out there to protect his woman. He felt he was leaving her as prey to his enemies. "I have the gift from Jefe. I will make sure things get handled. You just keep your word when you come home," China said as she looked at her watch. "I'ma let Spencer come back. I love you, and fucking call me!"

"I love you too, baby," Smooth said as he blew her a kiss. China blew a kiss back and then strutted off to go get Spencer.

When Smooth saw Spencer, he put his fist to the glass. Spencer placed his fist to the glass as well to show love.

"Thanks, man. You saved her from my problems," Smooth said.

"Don't worry, pal. You know we're on our A game," Spencer said as he then went on to inform Smooth about how Sue Rabbit and Guru were holding him down.

Smooth was shocked to hear that Spencer knew Sue Rabbit and Guru. He didn't want it like that, but he had little control over how things were happening now while he sat in jail. Smooth also told Spencer about Ham, to whom he wanted Spencer to pay a visit.

"I got you, bro," Spencer promised.

"Man, also I want you to stick by China's side until these muthafuckas are dealt with," Smooth ordered Spencer.

"I got you, Smooth, but I do have a question," Spencer said as he looked Smooth in his eyes. "China wants to be in on this cat. What's your say so?"

Smooth began chuckling, and Spencer laughed with him.

"Let her in. What she says goes!" Smooth said, much to Spencer's surprise.

"Are you sure she's . . ."

"Let her in. Don't underestimate China. She becomes very vicious when you do," Smooth warned Spencer. "Before you leave, call 772-634-3208 and ask for Meka. Then tell her to mail you all the information. Remember to bring China when you go. Keep her by your side like glue, Spencer."

"I will, bro. I got you ten toes down," Spencer added.

* * *

Amanda waited patiently for her doctor to come back into the room and go over her checkup results. She was on her iPhone playing PacMan, when an incoming call from Smooth chimed in and interrupted her game.

"Shit!" Amanda exclaimed as she hit the ignore button, refusing another one of Smooth's calls.

She felt that when she sat down face-to-face with him, they would have a more genuine talk about China and him.

He had no choice or say about their new relationship status. She was tired and refused to set herself up to get hurt. Smooth had to make up his mind, and she would help him do so, even if she had to enforce it by cutting him off.

"Good morning, Ms. Lewis," Dr. Lewis said as she walked into the room.

When Amanda looked up and saw the odd look on her doctor's face, she knew something was wrong.

"Good morning. Is something wrong?"

"Ms. Lewis, your tests came back. I'm sorry to tell you this, but you tested positive for HIV."

"What do you mean? You're kidding me, right?" Amanda chuckled briefly.

"No ma'am. I take my job and patients seriously."

"Oh my gosh! No! Please don't tell me this is true!" Amanda broke down and cried into Dr. Rosa's arms.

Smooth! Oh my gosh! she thought, realizing that the only man she had been having sex with and loving had given her something that she couldn't cure.

"Life isn't fair. I don't deserve this!" Amanda continued to sob.

"Don't worry, Ms. Lewis. We will immediately treat you. But if you know who could have given you this, then you need to tell him to get tested," Dr. Rosa explained.

Smooth! I can't believe you did this to me! Amanda thought, deeply hurt by the troublesome news.

Amanda now wondered if Smooth even knew he was HIV positive.

And if he does, why did he choose me? I've been nothing but good to him! Amanda reflected.

After leaving the doctor's office, Amanda went home and cried herself into a great depressive state. She had cut herself off from the world only to focus on Smooth, who always had her heart skipping beats when they were around each other. Now she had no one to turn to for comfort. And the only one she did have to turn to was incarcerated. She knew that he had given her HIV, beyond any doubt, because he was the only man she had been sexually involved with in the past couple years.

Why, Smooth? she thought as she lay in bed.

She had changed her mind about going to see Smooth. To keep herself sane, she wanted nothing to do with him anymore. She was done!

13

WHEN CHINA MADE it back to Miami and ditched Spencer, she drove over to GaGa's house, where she met Sue Rabbit and Roxy. Sue and Roxy were happy to see China when she pulled up and stepped out of Smooth's stash car.

"Shouldn't you be somewhere resting instead of out and about?" Roxy said as they walked inside, leaving Sue Rabbit in his car.

"I'm okay. If I needed rest, then I would have been asleep in bed."

Roxy and China both found GaGa in the kitchen preparing dinner. She was sitting at her kitchen table cutting collard greens.

"Hi, Mom!" China said as she hugged her.

"Woman, you will run a sista's blood pressure to the roof!" GaGa said.

"Please don't stress. Your daughter is fine, Mom!"

"Tell Sue Rabbit that he can come in. It's rude to keep your man outside," GaGa said.

"He's alright."

"I'll tell him," China said as she stormed out of the kitchen and back outside to call for Sue Rabbit.

She found him on his iPhone, sitting in the driver's seat. China startled him when she rapped on the window.

"Damn! You sneaking up and almost got it, China," Sue Rabbit said as he let down the window and showed China his Glock .50.

"Whatever! First things first! I have one hundred kilos for you and Guru. Every time you guys need re-up, bring the money, and I'll go handle business. I'm doing this out of respect for you and Guru, in response to these Mexicans. Other than that, I wouldn't be doing it!" China explained.

"And I really appreciate you looking out for us, China. We just want to hold shit down for Smooth."

"Don't we all!" China said with a chuckle. "When we leave here, we will handle business. But first, my mom insists on your coming inside. She finds it rude," China said.

"Sure, I'll come inside," Sue Rabbit said as he exited his Range Rover and walked inside with China to help GaGa with dinner.

When dinner was ready, the foursome sat together at the kitchen table and enjoyed GaGa's delicious soul food. China thought about her and Roxy's days of growing up in the old home that GaGa refused to leave for a better view. GaGa was an old-school mother who had just adjusted to driving new-model luxury cars as opposed to old classics. China enjoyed the company of her mother as much as GaGa loved having both of her daughters in the same room.

Damn, Smooth! It would be so good to have you here with us, China thought, missing him to the extreme. She wished that she could hold him and smell his distinct scent. *Don't worry, baby. I'll make sure this snitch gets his day in hell!* China thought.

"I have some good news to tell everyone. Well, Sue Rabbit already knows, so it'll only be news to Mom and China," Roxy began.

"What? Are you pregnant now?" GaGa asked as she took of sip of water.

"No! She's having twins, Mom!" China said, causing everyone to laugh.

"Both of y'all are wrong!" Roxy said. "Me and Sue Rabbit are planning on opening up four more Roxy's restaurants."

"Wow! That's wonderful! Roxy's bringing in that much money? I would have never expected that!" GaGa said.

"That's what up, Roxy!" China said.

"Yeah, China. And you will be over one of them. You could run the place however you want to," Roxy said.

"Are you serious?" China asked.

"Dead serious!" Roxy replied.

China hopped out of her seat and ran around the table and hugged Roxy. GaGa and Sue Rabbit smiled at the two siblings. Seeing her two daughters happy truly delighted GaGa and warmed her heart. When she looked over and saw the smile on Sue's face, she just knew without a doubt that he was the right man for Roxy.

Lord, thank you for this day! GaGa thought.

* * *

The rest of the day, Smooth was in his own world, depressed after being hit with the news of the loss of his unborn child. To make matters worse, Amanda wasn't accepting any of his calls. It wasn't like her to just stop talking to him. Smooth was worried and thought that maybe she was sick.

But why would she refuse my calls instead of just accepting them and telling me? Smooth pondered as he lay on his top bunk while Rosco and Baby Dread played chess on the bottom bunk.

Smooth had informed Rosco about the loss of his unborn child and appreciated the support that Rosco had given him. And China could have been killed by his enemies, if it were not for Spencer being there to save her.

I owe that man big time, Smooth thought.

"Checkmate!" Baby Dread screamed.

Smooth was surprised and didn't believe that Baby Dread had finally checkmated Rosco, until he saw it with his own eyes.

"Well I'll be damned!" Rosco said, double-checking the board to see if he had a chance to swindle himself out of checkmate, but he did not.

Baby Dread had his queen face-to-face with Rosco's king, who couldn't defeat his cousin's queen because Baby Dread's rook was lined up protecting his queen.

"Checkmate!" Baby Dread shouted hysterically.

"Rematch!" Rosco said to Baby Dread as he began resetting the pieces.

"Baby Dread done finally got tired, old man!" Smooth said while still looking down at the two contenders.

"Yeah, I slipped and let him eat my rook and knight," Rosco explained.

"Can't be slipping, old man!"

"How 'bout you get your ass down here instead of cheering behind the scenes," Rosco challenged.

"I will after I get off the phone," Smooth replied as he jumped down from the top bunk.

"Amanda still not picking up?"

"Still not picking up. That shit is crazy!" Smooth said to Rosco.

Rosco felt that Amanda was seeing someone else, but he didn't want to tell Smooth. Smooth also thought about that prospect, but he couldn't see it happening to him, especially after Amanda had declared how strong her love for him was.

Hell no! She isn't seeing anybody else! Smooth thought as he walked out of the cell to make a phone call.

Smooth picked up the phone and dialed Amanda's number. The phone rang twice, indicating that she had picked up. Smooth waited for the line to clear, but like lately, Amanda refused to accept the call.

Damn it, Amanda! What's wrong with you? Smooth thought angrily as he tried her number again, only to get the same results.

"Something's not right!" Smooth said as he then dialed Sue Rabbit's number.

Sue picked up his phone on the third ring, went through all the prompts, and then accepted the call.

"What's good, nigga?" Sue Rabbit spoke.

"Just cooling it, man. You tell me what's good!"

"Shit! I just left your mother-in-law's house with China and Roxy. GaGa put together a delicious dinner and got a nigga tank on swole," Sue Rabbit informed Smooth.

"Damn! I know how good that shit was. So tell me, did China holla at you?"

"Yeah, she really came through. We were on our last slow motion, canceling everything major, feel me?" Sue Rabbit said.

"Damn! I know what you mean. Y'all should be straight now. China will drive the ship like me. Feel me, Sue?"

"I feel you, bro," Sue Rabbit replied.

"My nigga, I got something else to ask you."

"What's that, bro?"

"When the last time you met up with Amanda?" Smooth asked.

"Shit! Last week, bro. She baked thirty for me and Guru."

"I've been trying to get a hold of her, bro, but she keeps blocking me out."

"She acting weird?" Sue Rabbit asked.

"Very strange!" Smooth informed him.

"I'll stop by and see what's up with her. How 'bout you give me a call in the morning, nigga, and I'll just drive over there," Sue Rabbit suggested.

"Yeah, that'll be cool, bro. Because I don't know what this bitch's problem is," Smooth said.

"Don't worry, bro."

"You have sixty seconds left," the automated voice chimed in.

"Bro! Get some rest. Don't sweat yourself."

"That's why I got mad love for you, man."

"The same over—"

"Thank you for using GTL," the automated voice said before disconnecting the line.

Well I guess I'll see what's going on in the morning, Smooth thought as he walked back to his cell to play a game of chess against Rosco.

"Did it work out?" Rosco asked.

"I'll find out in the morning."

"Well, that's progress. Now, get this ass-whipping," Rosco said.

"Whatever! Looks like Baby Dread done found your weakness," Smooth said as he sat down and began the game.

14

THE NEXT MORNING Smooth awoke anxious to get to the phone. It was 9:00 a.m., and he knew that Sue Rabbit was an early bird. Smooth climbed down out of the bunk and saw that Rosco was still asleep. They had talked each other to sleep last night about the beautiful women in Jamaica, a place where Smooth had never visited. He had promised to visit with China as soon as he was a free man again.

Smooth did his hygiene in a hurry without disturbing Rosco, and he then walked out to the phone area. Smooth first called Amanda's phone and got no answer. He then called Sue Rabbit, who picked up on the first ring and accepted his call after completing all the prompts.

"What's up, bro?" Smooth asked.

"Bad news, bro."

"What's going on, Sue?" Smooth asked, concerned about Amanda's safety now. He didn't know what to expect. He heard Sue Rabbit sigh before he spoke.

"I'm at the apartment, but she's not here."

There's a pad on the door, and neighbors said she moved out yesterday!" Sue exclaimed.

"Say what? Moved out? You sure she didn't move over to the trap? She said her neighbors were too nosey. So it wouldn't surprise me if she moved in the trap to lay low."

"Bro, she's not at the trap. I stopped there before I came here, to drop off some product," Sue Rabbit told him.

"Shit!" Smooth exclaimed angrily.

"This shit not adding up. Did you call her phone?"

"Three different times, bro! She's not picking up."

Could she be in trouble? Smooth thought. *Hell no. She moved out. But why?*

"Bro, I got a feeling that we need to be looking for another cook. Feel me?" Sue Rabbit suggested.

"Yeah, bro. Do you have anybody in mind?" Smooth asked.

"I have a couple, but they'll never spice it up like Amanda. She's the best I've ever seen."

"Tell me about it."

"You have sixty seconds left," the automated voice said.

"Keep your eyes open, bro. Even if you have to sit one of yo' lil niggas outside her front, door, do it!"

"Thank you for using GTL," the automated voice said before disconnecting the call.

Damn! Where the fuck is Amanda, and why is she acting the way she is? Smooth contemplated.

"No!" Smooth exclaimed when the prospect came to him of Amanda playing a role in setting him up too.

Could Amanda be down with Ham? Hell no! No way! I'm tripping. She was with me and walked inside the store, Smooth thought.

He knew he was thinking of an impossible prospect. It was something that was making Amanda run away.

Oh shit! She found out about China's pregnancy on the news. The entire Miami area heard that China had a miscarriage, Smooth thought, realizing what the only problem could be to cause Amanda to go mute on him.

"Damn it!" he exclaimed, kicking himself in the ass for not informing her that him and China expected a child.

"I fucked up! I really fucked up!" Smooth admitted as he picked up the phone to call China.

* * *

"Jenny Davis. Mail call!" the CO sorting mail announced. "Jenny Davis again! Mail call!"

Jenny came out of her cell and walked up to the table to grab her mail. When she saw that it was mail from China, she got excited and smelled the letter. China always sprayed perfume on her letters and cards. Jenny couldn't wait until she was able to wake up in the same bed every day with China and smell her addicting scent. Jenny saw that she had no more mail, so she strutted off back to her cell.

She sat down on her bottom bunk and tore open the first letter. Jenny felt a sharp pain in her chest when she read the first line: "I lost the baby."

"What the fuck happened?" Jenny asked herself as she continued to read China's heartbreaking letter.

China had put Jenny up on all that happened, and what she planned to do about it. Jenny was afraid for China's safety. She didn't want anything to happen to her. She loved China so much and couldn't stand to lose her to Smooth's enemies.

How could he put her in that situation where her damn life is at risk? Jenny wondered.

Jenny was too hurt and shaken up about the news to open up her second letter from China.

I hope she comes to see me soon. Maybe I can talk her into moving out of Miami, Jenny thought.

"Recreation! All inmates not assigned as house women, get out of the dorm and report to the recreation yard," the sergeant of the dorm exclaimed over the PA system.

"Just what I need. Some damn fresh air," Jenny said as she changed out of her uniform into her gym shorts, sports bra, and tennis shoes.

While she was bending over tying her shoes, Carlisha came into the cell and smacked her on her phat ass.

"You coming to watch me play softball, baby?" Carlisha asked.

"All day in America," Jenny replied as she gave Carlisha a quick kiss on the lips.

"It smells like China in here. I heard your name called for mail."

"Yeah, she lost our baby," Jenny said with tears forming in her eyes.

"Oh my gosh! I'm sorry to hear that," Carlisha said as she embraced Jenny.

Every day, Jenny talked about China's baby and how she couldn't wait to get home and be a family with China and Smooth.

"Don't let this bring you down."

"Someone tried to kill her too," Jenny explained while wiping her eyes.

"Damn! Is she okay?"

"Yeah, she said she made it out safe. Her only loss was the baby," Jenny explained.

"Let's just be glad that she's alive and not dead, baby. That means you three could still be a family, boo."

"You're right," Jenny said as she kissed Carlisha passionately. "I'll be a wreck without you, Carlisha. You're always here for me, and I'll never forget this, baby," Jenny said.

"I know you won't. Now come watch me kick some ass!" Carlisha said as they filed outside, where she would play softball.

* * *

When Smooth walked into the lawyer/client visitation room, he saw his lawyer, who had driven all the way from Miami to see him for the first time, since he had fired his

Martin County attorney. Mike Spruce was a middle-aged white man in his thirties, who was the best lawyer in Miami to go against the feds in a drug case.

"Nice meeting with you, Donavan. Sorry that I couldn't come sooner, but before I do come see my clients on the first visit, I study their case thoroughly to know what I'm dealing with. I was hired by your girlfriend, China Preston, and it only took me a day to get acquainted with this case. And from what I've read thus far, the reliance of the case—for the most part—will fall on their CI, whoever it is. My first motion will be to force the state to reveal the CI so we can see the background of him or her and see how credible the CI is, if the CI takes the stand," Spruce explained to Smooth.

"So how soon will you present this motion to the court?" Smooth asked.

"As soon as possible."

"Without this CI, does the state have a case to continue with the prosecution?" Smooth asked.

"Will they have a case without a CI?" Spruce said, with a laugh. "The same rules still apply. No CI, no case."

I like him already, Smooth thought. "What about the drugs?"

"What about probable cause?" Spruce replied.

"I figured that was the same case here," Smooth said.

"This is Florida. A lot of laws in Florida make the state hate themselves at the end of the day," Spruce said.

"So tell me, are you looking for a trial or a good deal?" Spruce asked Smooth.

"Sir, I'm looking to go home, not prison," Smooth announced.

"I got you, Donavan. Just watch me destroy them. You do your job, and I will do mine," Spruce said as he leaned in toward Smooth for more privacy. "Let's remember. No CI, no case. I will not go to trial with a CI. Do you understand me?" Spruce asked Smooth.

Smooth knew exactly what his lawyer was talking about. It was Smooth's responsibility to get rid of the CI. He just prayed that Ham was the only CI on his case that he had to worry about.

Could Amanda be an informer? Hell naw! Smooth thought.

Smooth looked his lawyer in his eyes and told him, "I got you, sir. I will do my part. You just do yours."

Spruce offered his hand, and Smooth shook it.

"I will, Donavan. I will," Spruce said.

* * *

Mall sat at the interrogation table again, listening to DEA agent Debrah Jones try her best to break him and get him to give up Smooth. After she had learned earlier today that the state was offering Mall forty-five years, she flew over to Metro-Dade Federal Holding. Mall was looking at a life sentence if he didn't settle for a deal. He didn't care. Snitching was against the damn code, and he refused to go out like a sucker. A lot of Smooth's people had turned state on each other, but they couldn't identify the man in the photos who consistently wore a hat. However, it took Mall one glance to know that it was Smooth. He played dumb and claimed never to have seen the man in the photo. But Debrah Jones was growing tired of everyone lying.

"Listen, Monroe. Why do you persist on lying to me about a man who's not even keeping it real with you? We hear the phone calls you make to Money, and we heard others selling out the boss."

"So, what does this have to do with me, ma'am?" Mall exploded, slamming his fist down on the table.

"It has a lot to do with you. Your life will be taken away while you rot in prison, because you don't want to give up the boss. We know that this man is your boss," Agent Jones said, pointing at Smooth's photo.

Mall began to chuckle, causing Agent Jones to get frustrated.

"Bitch! Listen!" Mall started, then "Awww shit!" he screamed when Jones came from under the table and sprayed him with pepper spray.

"I got yo' bitch, nigga. Burn in hell, fucker!" Agent Jones said as she departed the interrogation room, leaving a shrilling Mall behind and alone.

Agent Jones knew that the name of the man in the photo was Smooth. Too many people had given him up. Some knew him as the boss and others knew him as Smooth, but no data or agency could stumble across his government name.

"Agent Jones, don't worry yourself. Something tells me that we're getting real close," Jones's boss said to her while watching Mall burn from the pepper spray.

"I just hope so, boss," Jones said.

15

TINA STIRRED FROM her sleep when she heard someone rapping at the front door. She felt for Ham next to her and discovered that he was gone. She was used to it, and since the last incident of Ham choking her unconscious, she had refrained from asking him where he was running off to.

The knocking continued as she got out of bed and put on her gown that Ham had stripped off her when making love to her. Ham wanted to make love to Tina every time he planned on leaving. He was bringing in money, so she couldn't complain, and she even had access to his product. In spite of Meka catching her, Tina was back on drugs and didn't give a damn about the baby's safety. She was more eager to push the baby out, just to get done with carrying the extra pounds around.

One more damn month! Tina thought as she walked to the front door.

She unlocked the door and opened it. Her visitor was someone she had never seen before

"Excuse me, but is Ham home?" the beautiful woman asked.

"No, who the hell are you?"

Before Tina could finish, the woman punched her in her jaw and knocked her out.

"Bitch! You ask too many questions now!" China said as she stepped inside the apartment over Tina's unconscious body.

China dragged Tina's body out of the doorway and closed it behind her. In her hands, she carried a black duffel bag.

Inside were the tools she needed to finish the job she had come to do.

* * *

Marco and his M-13 brother Miguel got behind the gray Altima the moment it pulled out of Roxy's restaurant. The two women in the car had no clue they were being trailed. Marco was too far back at the first intersection to make his move. The two women were having a gleeful conversation, Marco observed. "They're very happy, esé!"

"Yeah, homes. I see that," Miguel said as he looked at his watch. "It's ten o'clock. This is the happy hour."

The light turned green, and the Altima took off, pushing past the forty-five-mile-per-hour speed limit. Before Marco could accelerate and follow suit, a Metro-Dade police cruiser came out of nowhere and put on its lights to pull over the Altima.

"Shit, esé! Why us, huh?" Marco exclaimed angrily as he slammed his hand on the steering wheel.

Marco passed the Altima that had pulled over to the side for a traffic stop.

"I say we still go at them and leave everything slumped, homes," Miguel suggested.

"We can't! The camera already has our tag if they replay the tape," Marco informed Miguel, who was a cold-blooded killer at just seventeen years old.

He was taking Jr.'s spot, and he was a more vicious killer than Jr. ever was.

"We'll catch them on another date. We can't crash out. They're less important. So let's remember that," Marco said as he turned off the main highway and found the first I-95 route heading north back to Fort Lauderdale.

* * *

"Bitch! How the hell you get pulled over?" Jane asked Tabby while they waited for the police officer to come up to the driver's side window.

"I didn't even see him," Tabby said, rubbing her huge stomach and turning down the radio.

When the police offer walked up to the driver, Tabby rolled down her window.

"What's the problem, Officer?" Tabby asked the handsome black officer who favored Tyrese Gibson.

Damn, he's fine as hell! Jane thought.

"Ma'am, this is a forty-five-mile-per-hour speed zone. Do you realize that you were going fifty-five miles per hour?"

"No, I didn't, sir. I'm just in a hurry to get home after a long day of work," Tabby replied.

"I can understand that, ma'am, but there are rules out here that we must follow," the officer said.

"Yes, you're correct," Tabby said as the officer shined his flashlight on Jane.

"Ma'am, why aren't you wearing your seatbelt? Don't you know that I can give you a ticket?" he said. "Let me see your license and registration. And you, ma'am, let me see your identification," the officer ordered.

"Damn, why do you have to be such an asshole. Let a bitch breathe!" Jane said, getting sassy with the officer.

The officer laughed briefly, finding Jane's smart-ass mouth amusing.

"I'll let you breathe alright," the officer said as he put his focus back on Tabby.

"You're not wearing your seatbelt either. And you're pregnant. Are you okay?"

"Sure, I'm okay. Like I said, mister, I'm tired from working," Tabby said with an attitude as she handed over her driver's license and car registration.

"Come on, ma'am. You too. I need your identification," he said to Jane.

Jane sucked her teeth, rolled her eyes at the officer, and then dug in her purse for her ID.

"Give this to him before I curse his ass out!" Jane said to Tabby as she handed her ID over.

Tabby grabbed Jane's card and handed it to the officer.

"Thank you, Ms. Sassy," he said as he strutted off to his squad car laughing to himself.

"Muthafucka thinks he's the king of the streets and shit!" Jane pouted.

"Girl, don't even let him get to you, like for real," Tabby said to Jane.

The officer came back to the car ten minutes later and handed back Tabby's license and registration.

"I'ma give you a break, driver. Jane Thompson, ma'am, I need you to step out of the car."

"Are you kidding me? For what?" Jane exclaimed as she watched the officer walk around to the passenger side.

He boldly opened Jane's door and then ordered her to step out again, with his hands resting on his .357 revolver. "Ma'am, could you please step out of the car."

"Girl, do what he says! I don't like how he's sounding," Tabby whispered to Jane.

Too many people have been being killed by police, and the smallest things have resulted in one's death, Tabby thought. She didn't want her friend to join the statistics of police shooting people for the wrong speculation. "Please, Jane. Just do what he says," Tabby whispered again.

Jane sucked her teeth and then stepped out of the car, staring into the officer's eyes. When he saw the hips and ass on Jane, his cock began to betray him.

"Ma'am, could you please walk over to my car and stand by the hood," the officer directed Jane while pointing toward his squad car.

"All this for not wearing a seatbelt?"

"Ma'am, again, please follow my orders!" the officer shouted.

Jane did as she was told. When she was standing in front of his car, he shined his flashlight into the car and looked at the passenger's floor and seat for anything illegal. He found nothing.

"Both of you have been to prison. The wrong police officer would do everything in his or her power to arrest your girl. Start teaching her to just keep her mouth closed," the officer said to Tabby as he slammed the passenger door.

Walking back to his car, he shined his light in Jane's face again, and then to her bulging red juicy tits.

"You're too beautiful to give me a hard time."

"What do you mean? You're the one getting on me about a seatbelt," Jane explained with an attitude.

"That's my job. Plus, I wasn't getting on nobody. I was only telling you what could happen to you. If I was a jackass, I'd give yo' ass a ticket more than your check. I could make it hard for you to pay your rent, and have you back into the system," the officer explained.

"What's your name?" Jane asked.

"My name is Officer Smith. Tyrone Smith, to be correct," he said.

"You like what you see, don't you?" Jane asked after seeing the lust in his eyes.

"I think you've very beautiful, like I've told you. Now that I have you away from yo' girl, I can speak what's on my mind."

"And what is that, Officer? Please tell me you fuck while using handcuffs, because I'm down for the kinky shit!" Jane said seductively.

"How kinky?"

"When do you get off?" Jane asked, avoiding Smith's question.

"I'll be off at twelve o'clock."

"Come to my place when you get off. Now let me go so I can get this hard day of work off me and put my kids to bed. I'll be waiting on you, Smith," Jane said as she dismissed herself.

Officer Smith watched Jane's ass sway as she walked back to the car and got inside.

"Damn! Come on twelve o'clock. I'ma fuck the shit out of that bitch," Smith said as he watched Tabby pull off and merge back into traffic.

Officer Smith felt like the luckiest man of the hour. Jane was a beautiful woman who could land a job as a model if she just knew the right people. And ten-year-veteran Officer Smith knew the right people.

* * *

When Ham passed by the Indiantown middle school on Farm Road, he never saw the unmarked SUV sitting in the school's bus ramp, until the car jumped behind him and threw on its red and blue lights.

"Fuck!" Ham screamed.

He had no license and had drugs and a gun inside the unregistered car. He was indecisive and was about to flee, until he heard Sgt. Running Man's voice come over the mic.

"Pull over, Hamilton. There's no need to flee."

Ham sighed in relief and then pulled over into the community park.

Sgt. Running Man killed his red and blue lights, pulled up alongside Ham, and then rolled down his passenger-side window.

"Don't you know that if the wrong police officer stops you, you're coming in with new charges," the sergeant said to Ham.

"I'm about to be a father."

"To an underage girl. We know all about Tina Scott, Hamilton. That's a dangerous responsibility, son!"

Ham remained speechless. It was time for him to listen now.

What else does he know that I thought no one knew? Ham thought.

"Who killed your cousin, Banga Hamilton?"

"I don't know who killed my cousin," Ham replied.

"You're lying to me, Hamilton. Let's remember, I'm on your side. There's no need to lie to me. If it wasn't for me, then you wouldn't be a free man."

No, if I didn't snitch on Smooth, then I wouldn't be a free man, Ham thought.

"I'm gonna ask you again. Who killed Banga to get him out of the way?" Sgt. Running Man asked.

"I think someone in Golden Gate did it. The big shot over there is Jason Dames," Ham explained.

He knew in his heart that Jason had something to do with Banga's death, because they were rivals and beginning to beef over turf before Banga was killed. Ham was just waiting to catch Jason solo and in possession of a lot of dope to make his move.

"Hamilton, try to stay out of Golden Gate. They're about to come down hard, and I don't need my CI getting caught up in the crossfire. Remember, we're always watching, son," the sergeant said as he drove off.

"Damn it, man! I fucking hate my life. How did it get like this?" Ham murmured to himself as he pulled out his crack pipe and took a hit before he pulled off.

He badly wanted to go find a trick and fuck the shit out of her, but he was close to home. He could just go home and make love to Tina. At least it would mean something.

When Ham pulled up to his apartment, he stashed his crack pipe in a hole in his ruined seat and exited the car. Ham walked up to his apartment and found the door unlocked.

"What the fuck! She left the door open." He then walked inside. "What the fuck!" Ham exclaimed when he saw his destroyed apartment. The worn-down sofa was turned over, and graffiti was on the walls. His heart dropped when he read the graffiti: Daddy, Save Me.

"Tina!" Ham screamed as he rushed to the bedroom with his gun in his shaking hands.

When he entered the dark room, he flicked on the light switch and lost all the air in his body.

"Tina! No, no baby!" Ham cried as he stared at a dead Tina on the bed with her throat cut from ear to ear.

When he looked at her bloody stomach that was cut open and childless, Ham fainted and fell to the floor of the room. The sight of Tina's cut throat was one thing, but seeing that someone had cut out their baby was another thing, and too much for Ham to bear.

* * *

When Officer Smith pulled up to Jane's apartment in his luxurious Lexus SUV, he saw that the area was quiet and very low key. He stepped out of his car and walked up to Jane's apartment door. Before he could knock, the door opened, and Jane stood there in lustrous satin lingerie.

Damn! Smith thought while staring at Jane's gorgeous body.

"What, nigga? Do the cat got yo' tongue, or haven't you tasted some good pussy in a while?" Jane challenged Smith.

"I see you got a fly mouth year-round, huh?" Smith said as he stepped inside and took Jane in his arms.

"If my mouth is too much, how about you put something in it, Mr. Officer," Jane said seductively while rubbing on Smith's chest.

Smith placed his mouth to Jane's and kicked the door closed behind him with his foot. As he kissed her passionately, she tasted like apple candy. Smith picked her up and carried her over to the plush sofa where he lay her down.

"Mmmmm!" Jane softly moaned as Smith caressed her body with his tongue.

When he got to her wet mound, Jane arched her back and locked her legs around his neck.

Damn! This nigga can eat some pussy. He reminds me of Smooth, she reflected.

"Oh shit! I'm coming!" Jane purred.

She couldn't believe how fast he made her orgasm.

"I got to have this dick!" Jane said as she helped Smith out of his pants.

When she saw his enormous dick, she almost declined. His girth was extremely thick.

"Can you handle this big boy?" Smith asked.

"We'll see!" Jane said as she slowly straddled him and descended on his cock.

Oh my gosh! He's too big! Jane thought as she filled her wet mound halfway with his cock. Jane held onto his neck and rode Smith slowly until her pussy got accustomed to his cock.

"Damn, this dick feels good!" she purred to Smith, who was sucking on her erect nipples.

Got his ass! And I mean for the long haul! Jane thought, deciding that she would keep him around and not run him off like the rest of her victims.

Officer Smith fucked Jane long and hard for an hour, putting her to sleep. Immediately after, he gathered his clothes and ran home to his wife and kids. He was hooked like she was, and yet another victim.

16

AFTER SEEING THE gruesome act of China taking the baby out of Tina's stomach, Spencer knew that he had met his equal in another gender. She was strikingly beautiful, and no one would ever expect her to be a cold-blooded killer. The infant was a crack baby, and it hurt China to her heart to see how nonchalant Tina was toward the baby's life. He was just a little boy who would never see his mom and dad.

Shit! They didn't deserve him! China thought.

"So you're really going to keep the baby?" Spencer asked China, who held the sleeping baby boy in her hands.

He was a bitty thing weighing only 4.1 pounds flat. He shook constantly and had a constant running nose. It was evident that the baby needed some serious medical assistance.

"I can't. It'll be too much of a risk," China said to Spencer, who had pulled into a 7-Eleven gas station to fuel up.

"So why did you bring him?" Spencer asked.

"So he wouldn't die! Don't worry about why I did what I did, Spencer, okay?"

Spencer looked at China and saw the hurt in her eyes. She had two much passion for kids to kill them. Spencer was another story. If the kid was part of the mission, then the kid would be wiped out. Spencer could have killed Ham the moment he showed up at the apartment, but he preferred to save the kill for another day.

China could feel Spencer staring her down while she fed the baby a bottle of powdered milk. When he didn't respond and stepped out of the car, China looked at his back as he walked into the 7-Eleven. She could tell that he was not feeling her decision, but she didn't care. She was the head of the ship, and what she said or did was final. She didn't need anyone to question her, and she was sure that Spencer now understood that.

They were on their way back to Miami to lay low until the heat of Tina's death died down. Both Spencer and China knew Ham wouldn't call the police. Tina was a minor and would bring unwanted attention to him that he could not afford.

When Spencer came out of the 7-Eleven and pumped the gas, he got into the Camaro and surprised China with a bag of junk food and a cold Pepsi.

"I thought you'd be hungry, so I got you something. There wasn't anything inside for him, or else I would have gotten him something for the ride too," Spencer said.

"Thanks, Spencer. Don't worry about him. All he needs is some milk, and I'm sorry if I sounded rude before."

"No need to apologize, China. What's unsaid is better understood than being said," Spencer replied as he pulled off from the 7-Eleven and hopped onto the I-95 heading south.

* * *

Ham had no clue who would have killed Tina and stolen their child. His confrontation with Meka wasn't enough to suspect her; besides, she was his cousin and cared for Tina. He was afraid to call the police, because they would suspect him and find out that Tina was a minor. To avoid prosecution, Ham chopped Tina's body into fractions, stuffed them into garbage bags, and threw them in a deep freezer.

Ham then began cleaning the bedroom, doing everything he could to get rid of the crime scene. Getting rid of the graffiti on the walls was the hardest because he was indecisive as to whether he should scrub the walls clean or paint over them.

After scrubbing to no avail, Ham decided to scrape the paint off and repaint the walls when the stores opened for the day.

Ham worked until the first sight of dawn, and then he got into his Chevy and drove into town to the first Home Depot, where he purchased many cans of white paint. At no time during the trip to and from the store did he ever notice the black SUV trailing him. He was too high and depressed to notice any threat toward him. All that was on his mind was finding the killer who had taken his love away from him. But he had no direction, and it deeply troubled him.

* * *

Sue Rabbit stepped out of the shower at dawn after a long and busy night at the trap house, where he was assisting the new cooker with preparing fifty kilos. Their cooker was an old-school woman referred by Big Mitch before he was arrested. It was someone Big Mitch had told Sue Rabbit would be suitable in case a rainy day ever came. Her name was Cookie, but she preferred to be called Auntie. She didn't have a touch like Amanda, who no one had seen, but she had what it took to keep the fiends and clientele coming. And that's all that mattered to Sue Rabbit and Guru.

Sue Rabbit dried his face and head while standing in the mirror. When he looked in the mirror, he almost jumped out of his skin when he saw Roxy standing behind him.

"Damn, baby! You can't be doing that," Sue Rabbit said, pulling Roxy into his arms. "Plus, I thought you were sleeping."

"I was until I smelled your aftershave," Roxy said as she caressed his smooth baby face.

"Oh yeah?" Sue Rabbit replied as he began sucking on Roxy's neck, making her giggle from his titillation.

"Boy, you know that shit tickles and turns me on!"

"Shit! What you think I'm trying to do?" Sue Rabbit said as he resumed sucking on Roxy's neck.

"Mmmm!" Roxy moaned, letting her robe fall to the floor, revealing her flawless nude body.

Roxy reached down and began stroking Sue Rabbit's erect cock with both hands. Without warning, she squatted and began sucking on his dick.

"Damn!" Sue Rabbit moaned as he looked down at Roxy sucking his cock with great passion.

"Mmmm!" Roxy moaned, twirling her tongue around the head of Sue's throbbing cock.

Roxy knew that she was doing her thing and making Sue Rabbit's head spin. He then grabbed the back of her head and began fucking her mouth.

"Mmmm!" Roxy moaned out as Sue's cock hit the back of her throat.

Before he could come to his climax, Roxy pulled away and stood to her feet. She turned around and ran out of the bedroom.

"Hide and go fuck!" she screamed.

Sue Rabbit followed after her, hopped in bed with her, and buried his head between her legs. He sucked on her throbbing clit and had her coming five minutes later.

"Damn, Trayvon. I love you!" Roxy purred loudly.

"I love you too, baby," Sue Rabbit replied.

After sucking up her juices, Sue Rabbit climbed on top of her and slowly entered her wet mound.

"Mmmm! Daddy, fuck me!" Roxy demanded, wrapping her legs around Sue Rabbit. "You love me, Trayvon?" Roxy asked in a purr.

"Yes, ma! I do," Sue Rabbit replied as he increased the strokes, going deeper with each thrust.

Every time he was inside Roxy, he felt like the luckiest man in the world. He dumped all his sideline sexual partners to be with her, and he was now ready to take it to the next level in life. He was ready to leave the game alone, but before he did, he wanted them to be financially stable for generations. Sue Rabbit knew that the dope game wasn't a job that would last forever. The statistics of trying it and failing were higher than succeeding.

Roxy felt Sue Rabbit deep in her womb and thought about what his reaction would be when she told him the news—the wonderful news. Just then, a tear escaped her eye and rolled down her face. When Sue Rabbit saw the tear, he licked the side of her face and kissed her as he continued to make love to her.

"Us against the world, baby!" Sue Rabbit whispered into Roxy's ear.

As if on cue, they both came to an electrifying orgasm together.

* * *

As soon as Smooth awoke, he did his hygiene and then dug in his locker for a quick breakfast. He never ate the jailhouse food. China kept his inmate account loaded to the point that he could pay for the entire jail's breakfast if he wanted.

Smooth grabbed himself a honey bun and a package of apple-flavored oatmeal. He took a peanut butter squeeze and squirted it all over the honey bun while he waited for the water to boil. As he ate the honey bun, he thought about Amanda. She was no longer picking up the phone.

She must have changed her number, Smooth thought, shaking his head.

It was crazy, and it made no sense to him how a woman could declare her love for a man but scatter at the first disappointment. Smooth remembered of all their good times, and seeing her smile always brought joy to his heart. It confirmed that despite their age difference, he was doing something good and not wrong. She had made a lot of money with Smooth by being his cook girl.

Is that what it was? The bitch saw that a nigga couldn't profit her like I could if I was out? Hell no! I can't see her playing a cutthroat game like that, Smooth thought as he swallowed his oatmeal and then walked over to the phones.

He dialed China's number and got her on the second ring. China accepted the call after all the automated prompts.

"Good morning, daddy," China's sexy voice spilled into Smooth's ear, putting a smile on his face.

"Good morning, beautiful. What's up with you? You sound like you're in a good mood. Tell me about it," Smooth said to her in code.

"Everything went well. I don't want to go into details, but we still have work to do."

"What do you mean?" Smooth asked.

"I did her. He decided to do him on a later date," China explained.

The line was silent, and China could sense that Smooth was completely lost.

"Baby, don't rack your brain! Just let us handle this shit out here," China said at the same time the crack baby started to cry.

What the fuck! A baby? Smooth thought.

"China, baby. Whose kid is there with you?"

"Let's just say right now he's ours if I decide to keep him. Like I said, I handled her, and he decided to handle him at a later date. Now let's get off this subject. How do you like your lawyer?"

"He made it clear that we need him handled."

"And he will, baby. I promise."

"I know," Smooth replied, letting China know that he trusted her to make sure Ham was dealt with.

He still had no clue that China had ripped a woman's baby from her womb a month before the baby was due, after cutting her throat.

"I miss you so much, Smooth," China said while feeding the baby a bottle of milk.

"Don't worry, baby. Daddy will be back out there. Listen, I need you to drop off a payment for my boy Stone Bolt. Can you do that for me?" Smooth asked China.

"Yes, baby. If that's what you want me to do. I will handle it after I go pick up Zorro and grab the rent money from Jane," China told him.

"Appreciate it, baby."

"How much do you want me to drop on him?"

"Drop $1,500 in his account and tell him to keep his head up," Smooth directed China.

"Okay, baby. I will."

"You have sixty seconds left," the automated voice announced.

"I love you, baby, and tell GaGa and Roxy that I love them too," Smooth said.

"I will tell them, baby. I love you too."

"Thank you for using GTL," the automated voice said before disconnecting the call.

Damn! I can't wait to get up out of this shit! Who the fuck's baby does China have that she's contemplating on making ours? She says she handled her. Her? Oh shit! Ham's baby mama, Tina! Smooth concluded.

The pieces were coming together now and were transparent for Smooth. To confirm his speculation, he was eager to pick up the phone; however, this time he dialed Spencer's number and got him on the third ring, after going through the prompts.

"What's up, Smooth?"

"Shit! You tell me what's going new? I hear you was in contact last night," Smooth said, getting straight to the point.

"So, you've already talked with China!" Spencer said.

"Yeah, and a toddler was doing all the damn talking. Please enlighten me."

Before Smooth could finish, Spencer exploded in laughter.

"What's so funny, Spencer?" Smooth inquired.

"Because, I don't know how to tell you that your girl has me beat when it comes to pulling the truth out of people," Spencer admitted.

"I'm still lost here, Spencer. Talk to me!" Smooth said, growing agitated.

Spencer stopped laughing and thought of the best way in which he could tell Smooth about a murder over the phone.

"Your girl did her first hands-on delivery, bro!" Spencer said, getting a silent line for half a minute.

"Damn!" Smooth said with a sigh.

"Yeah, bro. That's what I said. She definitely has me beat!" Spencer said, biting into an apple.

"So I'm guessing you have plans for buddy?" Smooth asked Spencer about his intentions with how he was going to handle Ham.

Spencer swallowed his chewed apple and then spoke. "Yeah. I have good plans for buddy. Just know that everything is under control, Smooth," Spencer said as he took another bite. "I'm going to have fun with buddy."

"Good, bro. I knew that I could count on you."

"I'm here, Smooth."

"You have sixty seconds left," the automated voice announced.

"All you need to do is work out and think about the first thing you're gonna do when you come home."

"Thank you for using GTL," the automated voice said.

"Shit! The first thing I'ma do when I come home is make sweet love to my baby," Smooth said as he walked into his cell where he found Rosco praying on his knees.

Rosco prayed every morning his feet hit the ground.

Smooth silently climbed on top and lay down. The moment he closed his eyes, a CO came over the loudspeaker.

"Johnson visitation. Booth number twenty."

Who the hell is this? It's gotta be Meka because China is in Miami, Smooth thought as he climbed back down from the top bunk, put on his boots, and then walked out of the cell.

Rosco was still in prayer, and Baby Dread was waiting for him to finish up.

When Smooth made it to booth twenty and saw his visitor, his heart dropped, and anger quickly overtook him as he snatched up the phone.

"Amanda, what the fuck is going on with you? Why aren't you accepting my calls and then—"

"Changed my muthafucking number on your ass? Smooth! You lied to me! Yo' ass was about to be a father, and you couldn't be a man to tell me about it."

So that's why she tripping! Smooth thought.

"Don't ask me what's wrong with me, Smooth! What's wrong is that I gave the wrong nigga my heart, and now it's costing me my damn life!"

"What the fuck you talking crazy for? Yo' life's not worth the wrong speculation!" Smooth snapped.

Amanda began breaking down like he had never seen her do before. It was evident to Smooth and anyone who was looking in on the duo that she was hurt.

"Baby, listen."

"No, Smooth. You listen! For years, you're the only man I've been sleeping with, loving, and caring about," Amanda said, putting up her fingers one, two, three. "And I've run all my friends off because I was too caught up in playing number two to a man who would have never made me his number one. All for what, Smooth? For my checkup test to come back positive for HIV!"

The words hit Smooth hard. *HIV!* he thought, now seeing why Amanda had lost weight. *Oh shit! That means I could be infected.*

"Amanda, are you kidding me?" Smooth asked.

Amanda looked up at him and laughed, and then told him straight up, "Go get tested and thank the bitch who gave it to you. And by the way, thank you for taking my life away. Have a nice life, Smooth," Amanda said as she hung up the phone and walked away without looking back.

Smooth was speechless and, for the first time in a long time, scared.

17

WHEN SMOOTH RETURNED to the dorm, Rosco could see the discomfort all over his face. Other inmates also noticed that his visit was the shortest ever. When he walked into the cell, Baby Dread and Rosco continued to play chess and eat honey buns with peanut butter topping. Like Smooth, neither Rosco nor Baby Dread woke up early to eat the jail's breakfast, even though it was better than most in other jails in Florida. Smooth hopped on his top bunk and leaned back against the wall.

Amanda's HIV positive, and she claims it came from me—her reason for avoiding me, Smooth thought, replaying the visit in his mind.

Seeing Amanda walk away, Smooth just knew that he would never see her again.

Lord, how can this be? Smooth asked the Most High as a tear rolled down his face. *Could China be infected if I'm infected? No! The doctors would have told China during her pregnancy if she had HIV, and after she lost the baby. If China doesn't have HIV, that means I caught it from someone after her, but who? Jane?* Smooth thought, after realizing who it was he had sex with other than Amanda and China.

Everything was coming back to him. He had stopped having sex with random women when China came home. He was only involved with Amanda. The last woman he had sex with other than Amanda was Jane. He and China had been on bad terms despite getting back together, but he never made it back to her to have makeup sex.

That's why China isn't HIV positive, Smooth concluded. *But could Amanda be blaming me as the one that infected her to take the burden off of her?*

I sexed Meka too. I gotta get tested! Smooth thought as he wiped away the tears that inevitably fell from his eyes.

He had written to Jane last week requesting that she send him some bikini pictures, but she hadn't responded yet.

Damn! How the fuck did I let this happen to me? Smooth wanted to know. When he reflected on all the many women he had unprotected sex with while China was in prison, he had no one to blame but himself if he had HIV. It was hard for him to accept that there was a high change that he did.

But how could I not be if Amanda is? he thought.

* * *

Guru had pulled up to the 7-Eleven gas station on the far side, away from the cameras. He saw that his client hadn't arrived, so he sparked up a phat-ass dro blunt. Emanating from his radio was an old throwback hit by Biggy Smalls. Ten minutes had gone by, and his connect still wasn't at the station.

"What the fuck! He was supposed to be here already!" Guru said as he looked at his Rolex.

Guru pulled out his iPhone and called his client, who picked up on the second ring.

"Hello?"

"Man, what's up? I've been at the station almost fifteen minutes, bro. Are you near or what?" Guru asked his client.

"Yeah, I'm pulling up now, homie. Just chill!" Guru's client told him, right when he pulled up alongside Guru.

Guru's client was a fisherman from the Keys named Cranmer, who was a six foot four, 225-pound Russian in his sixties, who caught sharks for a living. He stuffed the sharks with bricks of cocaine and trafficked them to another fisherman out of state. Sometimes, Cranmer would ship the stuffed sharks by water to other islands.

Guru had met him at a seafood restaurant at which Landi and he were eating, and Cranmer expressed his interest in cocaine. At first, Guru moved cautiously with Cranmer, just in case he was the FBI. But when Cranmer assured Guru that he wasn't a cop and offered to sell him weapons, Guru took the chance. When Cranmer got out of his SUV, he opened up Guru's passenger door and hopped inside with two duffel bags of money.

"Damn! It took you long enough, old man!" Guru said as he passed his blunt to Cranmer, who took it and inhaled deeply.

"I had to ditch a Metro-Dade cruiser. He wouldn't get off my ass until I started following him," Cranmer said. "I can't afford a stop in Miami. I hate coming through here."

"Don't worry. The next two drops, I'll come to your neck of the woods," Guru said.

"Good! That'll be great. I'll have some good shark meat for you and your girl. I speared one of them fuckers today, and I tell ya, that boy has enough meat on him to feed Haiti alone," Cranmer explained.

"That'll be nice, Cranmer. We'll be down there the end of the month," Guru promised as he reached into the backseat and retrieved two duffel bags, each stacked with fifteen kilos of cocaine each.

He tossed the bags onto Cranmer's lap and tossed the money into the backseat.

"I've run across some more AK-47s too, so when you come, make some room for them to go back with you."

"How many do you have?" Guru asked.

"Fifteen of them are yours, buddy," Cranmer promised.

"That's why I like you, old man. You're always coming through for the boy," Guru expressed.

"Hey, you're always looking out, so I have to show the same back. It's all appreciative business and washing each other's back."

"Hey, I ain't washing yo' hairy back, old man!" Guru said, causing Cranmer to chuckle.

"Nice one, bud. See you at the end of the month," Cranmer said as he passed back Guru's blunt and then exited his SUV.

Guru and Cranmer were both satisfied as they pulled off in opposite directions.

Guru showed up at Roxy's restaurant in time to get some breakfast. He ordered takeout for two separate orders, one for him and one for Landi, who was waiting for him to return to their condo. Roxy had prepared his order and thanked him for choosing her restaurant. Guru got back into his Lexus, opened up his bag, and stuffed his mouth with a hash brown.

"Now that's a hash brown!" Guru savored it.

There was no doubt that Guru had the munchies from the dro blunt. As he pulled out into traffic, he turned up his music, never seeing the black Suburban two cars back.

When he came to the red light at the intersection, he was sandwiched between two cars. The Suburban pulled up, and it all happened too fast for Guru. He could only duck from the rapid shots of the AK-47 that rang out from the Mexican who was hanging out of the passenger window. The Mexican sprayed into the Lexus SUV, hitting a ducking Guru in his back and legs. Guru had no chance to respond. The shots stopped, and he could hear tires burn out.

The pain from the shots was unbearable. As he lay there and his world got dark, all he could think about was Landi telling him to back out of the game. *I wish I would have done it earlier, because now it is too late*, Guru thought as his world came to a complete stop. He could hear nothing nor feel his life any longer. When the Metro-Dade police pulled up to the scene, they found Guru unresponsive.

"Victim is a black male in his twenties. Shot multiple times. Seems to be unresponsive," the Metro-Dade police officer said into his radio.

"Fifty-four! Paramedics on their way, sir," dispatch responded.

"Ten-four!"

* * *

"He tried to run, esé! Did you see him?" Miguel shouted to Marco, who was still racing through traffic, trying to find the first I-95 ramp to head back to Fort Lauderdale.

Miguel's adrenaline was racing one hundred miles per hour after releasing an entire fifty-round clip in the nigga he knew was rocking with Smooth. He had seen Guru numerous times on Smooth's block, so he knew that the dude was a target. Any man coming from Smooth's block was a threat to him and his M-13 brothers.

"I just wish that was Smooth's ass, Miguel."

"That would mean it would be a cold day in hell, Marco," Miguel replied logically.

Marco also knew that it was impossible for anyone to catch Smooth.

Shit! Catching China seems to be a pain in the ass for them too, they both thought.

"If we catch these muthafuckas one by one, esé, then we making a muthafucka feel M-13," Miguel said.

"That's why I like you, Miguel. You're a young soldier that knows the art of war," Marco said as he merged onto I-95 northbound.

"We just gotta keep our eyes open, because she's out here," Marco reminded Miguel, who was loading another fifty-round clip into his AK-47, which was still warm from spraying his slipping foe.

It was Miguel who spotted the familiar face walking out of Roxy's restaurant. All week he had been itching to kill someone, and his opportunity had finally come for him. And like he always did, he cocked back, aimed, and fired. He had no doubt that the dude was out for the count. He wanted to hop out of the Suburban, but his better judgment told him to trust his shot and have faith that he had taken out one of Smooth's guys. Neither Marco nor Miguel was aware that the man that had been gunned down was an important man who was third in Smooth's operation. The retaliation heading their way was something that neither would ever expect.

"Good job, Miguel!" Marco said proudly of his brother.

"M-13 homies *por vida!*" Miguel replied, throwing up their M-13 gang sign with his hand.

* * *

China decided to take care of Stone before she drove over to Miranda's to pick up Zorro. When she stepped out of the newly painted smoke-grey Benz, the sun licked at her skin. She had left the baby with a hired nanny named Amber for a couple hours while she handed her business.

"Damn! It's hot as hell out here!" China complained as she walked toward the jail's entrance.

The black tights hugged her curves lustrously and had the lust-filled eyes of the men hissing at her like a snake.

Get a fucking life! China thought, ignoring them.

When China walked inside, she sighed, since it was much cooler and more comfortable indoors. She searched the lobby and found the money machine with two people, a woman and an old man, standing in line to use it.

I'll check in first, China decided.

She stepped up to the young receptionist, who immediately got to her.

"May I help you?" the receptionist said into the mic.

Damn! She sounds just like Tracy, China thought.

"Yes, I'm here to visit Stone Bolt."

The receptionist gave China an ill look that disturbed her.

"What! Do you have a problem or something? If you one of his hoochie mamas, I'm not concerned," China said to the receptionist before rolling her eyes.

"Whatever, woman! Save that shit for Stone, not me. Anyways, booth 12 is where he will find you," the receptionist said rudely and then clicked off her mic.

"Bitch, if I ever catch you, I'ma give it to yo' ass!" China said as she walked over to the money machine where she inserted $1,500, just as Smooth had instructed her to do.

She then walked back to the visitation area and found Stone waiting for her. He seemed surprised to see China, and it took him everything he knew to bridle his instant lust for her.

"What's up, gal?"

"Listen, I'm only here because Smooth wanted me to drop off some cash and put it on your books. There's $1,500 on there, so you have money for canteen, which I'm sure that you're doing good without that."

"The mon is doing straight, but not on friends' accountability," Stone said.

"Damn! That's fucked up!" China replied.

"Yeah, and these niggas are singing like Beyoncé."

"Really?"

"Yeah, mon. Detectives want me to hand over Smooth. They know him, but nobody knows his first name," Stone informed China.

"So muthafuckas saying his name and trying to snitch, huh?" she inquired.

"Too many, and they're out on the bricks. So you tell Smooth to continue to lay low."

"He's fine. Do you know some of these snitching-ass niggas? Where they are?" China asked.

Stone looked at China and saw the cold-blooded look in her eyes. He knew a down bitch when he saw one. He admired her and saw Smooth as a lucky man.

If only she was mine, Stone thought before he spoke.

"A lot of my men have flawed me out. They're on 12th in Little Haiti, and Smooth's men are on bond, except for Money. This news came from my connections," Stone said.

He has no clue that Smooth is incarcerated, China thought.

"Baby gal, move safe out there, and tell my boy that I said what's up. I'ma take mines like a G is supposed to, mon. Me never give thee police any time of thee day, mon!" Stone informed China.

"Thanks, Stone. We'll always be here for you," China said as she stood up. "You just keep your head up, okay?" she added as she put her fist to the glass.

"I will, mon. Thanks," Stone replied as he put his fist to hers.

"See you later, Stone," China said as she hung up the phone and walked out of the visitation lobby.

Stone stayed in his seat and watched her lustrous ass sway from side to side.

Damn! That man has a bad bitch. I'd retire the game if I was him, before he ends up looking at a boatload of time, Stone thought before he got up to return to his dorm.

China couldn't believe how niggas were trying to turn over Smooth.

After all the love he has shown these muthafuckas, they want to try and backstab him! China thought as she got into her Benz.

When she checked her phone, she saw three missed calls and texts from Roxy.

"What does she want?" China said as she called Roxy's cell phone while pulling out of the jail property.

Roxy picked up on the second ring.

"China!" Roxy shouted in the phone.

"Yeah, what's up? Why you so damn—"

"Guru just got shot, down the street from the restaurant. Where are you, China? I'm worried," Roxy expressed.

"I'm leaving the jail. I'm on my way. Is he okay?" China asked.

"No, China! He had no chance!"

"Fuck! Where's Sue Rabbit?" China inquired.

"He's here with me. He's not taking it well, China. I need help. He's about to go headfirst. I see it all over him."

"That was his homeboy Roxy. Of course he's going headfirst. I'm almost there," China said as she hung up and headed to the restaurant.

As China accelerated through traffic, she called Miranda's phone.

"Hello," Miranda answered.

"Miranda. Sorry, but I'ma be a little late. Something came up. But if you got some place to be, I'll come get him right away."

"You're okay, China. Me and Zorro are having a great time together. I'm taking him for a walk now, so take your time."

"Thanks, Miranda," China said before she hung up.

China slowed down when the traffic backed up, and she immediately knew that it was because of the crime scene up ahead.

Damn! How the fuck did Guru get caught slipping? Smooth isn't going to like this one, China thought as she waited for the traffic to clear up.

Metro-Dade police were directing the traffic and doing their best to make sure the crime scene stayed secured without any wrecks occurring.

I wish Roxy would have been more detailed about where it happened, other than "down the street." I could have come from the other side, China thought as she slowly moved with the traffic.

It was a whole fifteen minutes before she was able to pass by the crime scene.

"Oh my gosh!" China exclaimed when she saw Guru's bullet-riddled Lexus SUV and a white shroud laid over his body, which hadn't been removed from the scene.

Damn it, Guru! China thought, realizing how it could have been Smooth in Guru's place.

At that moment, China could actually say she was happy to know exactly where Smooth was and grateful to know that he was safe rather than on his way to a body bag.

"Thank you, Lord," China said as she pulled into Roxy's parking lot, a place where she had almost lost her own life.

18

WHEN LANDI LEARNED of Guru's death, it was a bombshell
for which she wasn't prepared. The news came from one of
her coworkers, who worked as a policewoman on the road.
When she identified the victim as Landi's boyfriend, she
immediately called Landi, who had been waiting for Guru to
return from handling some business.

Landi had been growing worried and suspected perhaps
another DEA sweep, but not death. She had called out from
work to clear her mind. The murder was all over the local
news, but Landi still couldn't believe Guru was gone.

She was sitting in a redneck bar in downtown Miami
drinking whiskey, shot after shot. She wanted to get away
from the world and feel no more pain.

"Let me get another shot," Landi demanded.

"Ma'am, you're too damn crashed for another drink."

"Look here, fucker! Give me a drink before I make you
wish—"

"Look here, lady. Don't you threaten me! The policy says
I don't have to continue to sell you shit beyond intoxication,"
the bartender informed her.

"Fuck your policy, you redneck muthafucka!" Landi said
as she reached into her purse and removed her fully loaded
.380. "I want my drink, fucker!" She aimed her gun at the
muscle-bound man.

People in the vicinity slowly began leaving, not wanting
to be caught up in the life-and-death situation.

"Ma'am, you're ready to lose your life because of a
drink?" the bartender said as he walked toward her.

"Don't come closer! I will shoot!" Landi shouted.

The bartender froze in his tracks, afraid to take another step.

"It looks like you're in pain, lady. Maybe you've lost someone. I don't know"—the bartender shrugged his shoulders, "but it's not equal to going and ruining your life, whatever the case may be."

He knew that out of all the people leaving, someone was calling the police. At least he was praying for someone to have done what he would have done in the same situation.

"He was a good man to me. No one had ever treated me the way he did. And someone killed him today," Landi said, wiping tears from her face.

The loss of Guru was too much for her. She just wanted to be wherever his mind was, at the moment. No one in the bar understood her pain.

On the television in the bar, Landi saw the news update to Guru's murder.

"That's him!" Landi nodded her head toward the television. "He didn't deserve to die. I was at home waiting on him. I can't even tell him that he was about to be a father."

When the bartender looked at the news update, he froze and forgot all about his life being in danger.

"That's a nigga you're crying for!"

Boc! Boc! Boc! Boc!

Before the bartender could get out his insult, Landi lost it and pulled the trigger. The slugs hit him in his face and instantly killed him.

"Oh my gosh! What have I done?" Landi exclaimed when she saw the bartender fall to his death.

The entire bar went into a frenzy. Landi turned on her heels and fled the bar, stumbling from being so intoxicated.

"Murderer!" someone shouted.

Landi turned around and fired a shot in the air, causing more frantic behavior to erupt outside. Landi found her Altima and ran toward it.

I gotta get out of here! she thought as she reached for the driver's door.

"Freeze, lady! Put down the weapon! Metro-Dade police."

"Nooo!" Landi exclaimed as she turned around and saw three police officers aiming their guns at her.

"Why me, huh?" Landi shouted while holding the gun in her hand.

"Landi!" a police officer called out, immediately recognizing her.

When Landi looked at the young officer with her best blurry vision, she recognized him too. He had a crush on her, but he was always turned down.

Chad! Landi remembered his name. "Yes, Chad. It's me! What? Am I under arrest?" Landi asked, being sarcastic with him.

"Listen, Landi. Just put down the gun. Come on. You're one of us. We could talk things out and see what's going on," he said, trying his best to be a negotiator and get her to surrender.

"Chad, I loved him. I can't believe that he's gone."

"Landi, put down the weapon now!" a sergeant shouted to her.

Landi shook her head.

Sergeant Barns wasn't taking any chances. Chad wanted to tell Barns that he could handle Landi, but it was now out of his hands.

"Please, Landi! Don't get yourself—"

Boom! Boom! Boom! Boom!

Before Chad could warn her, Sergeant Barns fired his weapon and hit Landi high in her chest. As her body slid down the car, leaving a blood trail, she blinked her eyes twice and then took her last breath.

It was too much for Chad to see, so he closed his eyes to refrain from exploding on the sergeant.

"Suspect down and unresponsive. No longer a threat to the Metro-Dade Police Department," Sergeant Barns said over his radio to dispatch.

"Ten-four copy, sergeant," dispatch replied.

Sergeant Barns looked over at Chad, who was bridling his emotion, which Barns could clearly see. Sergeant Barns put a cigarette in his mouth and then spoke. "Are you going to be alright, son?"

Chad looked at Sergeant Barns and wanted to ask him why he killed her, but he knew that his job would be on the line.

"Yeah, I'm okay," he simply answered as he walked away to question witnesses.

I know you are, Sergeant Barns said to himself as he lit a cigarette while staring at Landi's lifeless body.

"Damn shame, girl!" Sergeant Barns said as he blew smoke down at Landi.

* * *

When Meka heard the news about Guru, she couldn't believe that another person she had known in her life was gone. Guru was someone she'd once had feelings for and had sex with, before she put her focus on Smooth. Smooth never knew, but if he had ever asked, Meka would have told him.

She had no clue when Smooth planned to take out Ham.

Maybe he's waiting for Ham to see the birth of his crack baby, Meka thought.

Since she had kicked out Ham's teeth, Meka hadn't been back to his place. Seeing Tina protect him had grossed her out. She was waiting for Smooth to make his move.

Because the sooner Smooth handles Ham, the sooner he'll be home, Meka thought as she sat on her sofa and ate her TV dinner.

Come morning, Meka planned to go visit Smooth and see if he was alright after hearing about Guru's death.

Damn! I hope he's alright! Meka thought as she turned the television to BET, where she watched a music video with Rihanna and Drake.

"Now that's a fine-ass nigga!" Meka said, admiring Drake.

She stood up and started dancing to the video.

"Work, work, work!" Meka sang the lyrics out loud, pretending to be dancing for Smooth.

Damn! I can't wait for his ass to get home. I swear I'ma put this pussy on him like never before, she thought as she watched the singers on the screen.

"Soon, baby! Real soon that nigga Ham will be history, even if I have to do it myself!"

* * *

"You ready for this shit?" China asked Sue Rabbit, who was sitting in the passenger seat of a stolen SUV.

"China, I live for this shit! It's not 'bout us no more. This shit 'bout Guru!" Sue said as he racked his MAC-10.

"Money, let's go!" China said to him over her walkie-talkie.

"I'm here," Money said.

China looked over at Sue Rabbit, and they both pulled ski masks over their faces.

"Let's go!" China announced as she exited the SUV with two fully loaded Glock .45s in her hands.

She and Sue Rabbit ran into the Mexican restaurant on 37th and began hitting random Mexicans.

Boom! Boom! Boom! Boom!

Money chopped down the men who escaped, and ran out the front door with his AK-47. The restaurant was another one of Juan's establishments that Mario was still running. Sue Rabbit and China ran toward the back of the place and found the office door locked. Sue Rabbit took a step back and ran toward the door with his shoulder, causing the wooden door to burst open. As he ducked and fired, China released a fusillade of shots, catching three frightened female cookers with deadly slugs.

"What? You bitches thought this was the hideout, huh?" China shouted.

She looked at Sue Rabbit, who pointed at the oak desk. Sue's signal to her was to take the opposite side of the desk while he took the other end. When China did, a Mexican sprung to his feet with a sword and swung at her head. She ducked on time and gave the Mexican a kick to his stomach. As he flew backward, Sue Rabbit shot him in the face.

"This muthafucka just tried to swipe my head off!" China said as she aimed at him and shot him twice more in his face.

* * *

Sue Rabbit called a meeting back at the trap house for all his lieutenants and sergeants to report with their workers under them. It was requested by China. She wanted to see everyone who was arrested on the 2100 block during the sweep and was out on bond. China looked at her G-Shock watch and saw that it was 4:00 a.m. She wanted to get her point across and then go home to rest.

"People, we are here to discuss some shit that needs to be addressed. Today we lost a soldier—an important soldier. And we're not done retaliating. Until Guru is laid to his final rest, we will give these Mexicans what they've earned," Sue Rabbit said while searching the faces of more than thirty men.

"Everyone that bonded out, step forward," China ordered her men.

Everyone in the room looked at one another, a little perplexed.

"I didn't stutter! Now, like I said!"

Boom! Boom! Boom! Boom!

"Those with bonds step forward," China demanded, after shooting a worker in his chest and face.

The other men in the room all wished they were never tricked into disarming themselves when coming to the trap house. They all smelled trouble, but the men who were out on bond stepped forward. The count came up to nineteen men in total. They were all workers, except for four of them.

"Smooth was good to all of you muthafuckas, and yet y'all betrayed him!" China said as she walked up to Sue Rabbit, who had opened a black case that concealed an AK-47.

China quickly grabbed the gun, racked it, and then stared at the frightened workers.

"Why? Somebody please tell me why a good man, and you muthafuckas are out trying to bring him down, huh?" China asked as she aimed at the workers and took down ten of them.

Sue Rabbit took down most of the other half and left all the workers slumped. The lieutenants and sergeants were all frightened, but they were solid.

Money sat among the ranked men with the same prospect of China running through his head that was running through theirs. China was a coldhearted, serious bitch that no man wanted to be against on the wrong side of the road.

She is nothing like Smooth, Money thought.

"Money! Get this mess cleaned up. I want all of them thrown into the Everglades," China ordered as she walked out of the soundproof trap house with Sue Rabbit on her heels.

Once outside, China stopped and turned to Sue Rabbit.

"Go home and lay low. The streets are going to be hot. I don't need you in them to get burned, Sue Rabbit," China said as she walked off and got into her Benz SUV.

"I got you, boss lady," Sue said as he departed from the trap house and headed home to his woman and true love.

When China got home, she rubbed the sleep from her eyes. She had had a long, stressful day. She badly wanted to hear Smooth's voice and express to him how much she was missing him. She needed him home with her, and out of the game. Seeing Guru get killed was a wake-up call itself, and she was hoping that Smooth saw the same prospect.

China looked up at the $2.3 million mansion and saw that they were living the American dream. Letting the streets take it from them was a waste of hard work.

Smooth, we've come so far into this game. It's time to give it up, baby, she thought as a tear escaped her right eye.

She didn't want to bury Smooth like she was about to contribute to bury Guru.

Damn it, Smooth! Please don't let me down!

"Oh shit!" China shouted, frightened by the two raps on her car window.

When she looked, she saw that it was Spencer. He was dressed in all black and wore a black skully on his head. She was pissed as she opened her door and stepped out.

"You must be out of your mind, Spencer! You scared the shit out of me!" China said while walking to her front door.

"Not really! I've been worried about you. Are you okay?" he asked.

The way he asked her out of concern put a smile on China's face. She thought that it was cute of him to be concerned. She knew that he had a thing for her, and to her, it was dangerous.

What does he want? It's almost five o'clock in the morning! China thought as she put her key in the door.

"I'm okay, Spencer. So tell me, what's on your mind?" she asked.

"There's a lot on my mind. I'm going back to Martin on Sunday night."

"Are you going, or are we going?" China asked, raising an eyebrow.

Spencer smiled impishly, going back to what Smooth had warned him about: not underestimating China.

"Of course *we* are going, China. I wouldn't leave you out of the fun for nothing in the world."

"Do you want to come in for some coffee? You look like you need it," China offered.

Spencer looked at his watch and then thought about the good offer. He definitely wanted to come inside, but he had a task to get to as soon as dawn rose.

"Thanks, but I have to handle something. Besides, you're the one who looks like she needs a strong cup of coffee," Spencer said, judging the redness in her eyes.

"I don't think so, Spencer. Don't do coffee at odd hours. Well, I guess I'll see you around. You know where to find me," China said as she opened the front door and met a happy

Zorro, who was jumping all over her like an excited kid. "See you later, Spencer."

When she turned around, he was gone. He had vanished into the night like a ghost.

"Damn it, Spencer! You're a smooth muthafucka!" China said as she shut the front door and set the house alarm.

She walked into the kitchen and refilled Zorro's water bowl and then fed him two cans of dog food. When Zorro was settled, China walked to the guest room and found her nanny asleep in bed with the crack baby, who slept peaceful yet with a perpetual shake.

"I hate your mama and daddy," China said to the baby, who she never gave a name.

Seeing him suffer from his parents' wrong decisions caused her pain every time she looked at him.

"I'ma call you Lucky. Because you're a lucky baby boy!" China whispered as she walked out of the room and closed the door, making sure not to wake the nanny or baby.

She walked into her bedroom and stripped out of her clothes. She walked into the bathroom and hopped into a hot shower. She was eager to hang with Spencer come Sunday. His presence comforted her and made her feel safe.

"Shit, how am I supposed to feel about a handsome man saving my life?" China asked herself.

At times she felt that she was being unfaithful to Smooth when she thought of how Spencer was making her feel.

But damn, how am I being unfaithful? Shit! When I was in prison, this nigga was fucking any bitch with a phat pussy! Why can't I have a friend if I decide to? Shit! I'ma ask Smooth just to see where his head is at. Will it be selfish or give me the green light? But, damn! Even if he does say yeah, I can't fuck the man's hit man! China thought with a smile on her face as she showered. *That's being too damn nasty, girl*, China thought to herself.

When China got out of the shower and dried off, she walked into the bedroom and found Zorro lying on top of her bed. She pulled back the comfy coverlet and hopped into bed nude.

She was so exhausted that she forgot to put her iPhone on its charger. As soon as her head hit the pillow, China was dozing off. In no time, she was dreaming of her and Smooth walking on the beach and holding hands. Her dream switched from the man she loved to the man for whom she was yearning—Spencer. She was in his strong arms and staring into his adorable loud blue eyes leaning toward her. When his lips touched hers, her body betrayed her, and she came to an orgasm.

"Mmmm!" China awoke moaning. "Spencer!" she called out as she continued to cum. "Oh my gosh!" China exclaimed as she shot up abruptly from her sleep, realizing that she had just had a wet dream.

China felt her throbbing clit and felt her wet pussy. She couldn't believe what she was going through.

"Damn! I need me some dick or a bitch!" China said, then played with her pussy until she came again, moaning out Smooth's name, wishing that he was giving her the loving her body was lacking.

19

WHEN SMOOTH HAD awoken and fed himself what he considered breakfast, he walked over to the phone. It was early, and only other person he was eager to hear from first thing in the morning was China. He had tried to get to sleep all night, but he couldn't after hearing Amanda's voice replay in his head repetitiously: "HIV positive."

Smooth had excluded China from being infected, but he wasn't sure about Meka and Jane.

The virus could have come from either of them, Smooth thought.

As he dialed China's number, her phone rang four times before her voicemail came on, "Hi, this is China. Ya girl's not available at the moment, so please just hit me back." Beep!

Smooth hung up the phone and redialed her number.

Maybe she's in the shower, Smooth thought as he listened to the phone ring persistently until the voicemail came on again.

"Hi, this is China—"

Smooth hung up the phone and immediately called Meka. Her phone range twice before she answered it and went through all the prompts.

"Good morning, baby," Meka said in a sexy voice.

"Good morning to you too, Meka. What are you doing up so early?"

"I'm getting ready for a job interview. Someone finally wants to hire a CNA."

"Where at?" Smooth inquired.

"Emerald in Port St. Lucie."

"Shit! That's good! So when will I see you?" Smooth asked.

"Damn! You're reading my mind, huh? I'm coming after my interview, so expect me at noon," Meka told him.

Damn! She sounds so healthy! Smooth thought.

Smooth's silence prompted Meka to question his plans.

"What? Are you expecting someone else to come see you today?"

"Nah, boo. Come through. Daddy ready to see you!" Smooth said, pouring music into Meka's ear.

He acts like he don't know shit about Guru, Meka thought.

"Smooth?"

"What's up, baby?"

"Have you heard about what happened yesterday?" she asked.

"Nah, yesterday! Where?" he said, coming alert.

He heard Meka sigh, and he immediately thought that she was about to confess to him about having HIV. But instead, she dropped a bombshell on him that he wasn't prepared to hear.

"Guru was killed yesterday morning in Miami."

"Say what?" Smooth shouted, not believing his ears.

"Yes, Smooth. It's everywhere in town," she informed him.

How? And I just talked to China yesterday morning! Smooth thought.

"Meka, let me go. I gotta check up with Sue Rabbit," Smooth said with grief in his voice.

Damn, he's hurt! she thought.

"Okay, baby. I'll be out there at noon to see you. Don't do nothing stupid!"

"I won't!"

"Promise me, Smooth."

"I promise. See you later," Smooth said as he hung up the phone.

"This shit can't be true!" Smooth said as he dialed Sue Rabbit's number.

He had no clue that he had disturbed a couple inmates who were sleeping when he shouted a moment ago.

Sue Rabbit's phone rang twice before he answered and went through the prompts to accept Smooth's call.

"What's good, bro?" Sue Rabbit said.

Smooth could tell that something was wrong with Sue. He just wished that Meka was somehow incorrect with her news.

"Tell me it's not so, Sue!" Smooth said.

He heard Sue Rabbit sniffle and could see in his mind the tears he was wiping away.

"He's gone, Smooth! Too fast and too young."

"Shit!" Smooth exclaimed in a whispered shout. "Who?"

"You already know who's aiming at us, bro. Them Mexicans not sleeping until we all in the dirt. We gotta get out while we can."

"What the fuck are you talking about, Sue? Just because they drop one of us, that don't mean we tuck our tails and bow down to them!" Smooth exclaimed.

"It's not 'bout tucking our tails, bro. It's about being a smart contender."

"Running from your enemy is smart, huh?" Smooth asked.

"Sue Rabbit runs from no man, Smooth. I'm out here with your lady holding down our turf and letting muthafuckas know that they can't get away with rolling over on you," Sue Rabbit exploded, not appreciating Smooth considering him to be running.

Every day he stepped out of the house, he was dodging Smooth's bullets and his own. He was ready to leave the game to the niggas who lived to play it. Smooth's mind was all fucked up thinking about what was occurring.

"Man, did we respond?"

"Yeah, we responded, and yo' lady washed a couple niggas on the team who were working for the DEA, trying to bring the whale down!" Sue Rabbit explained.

"Where did this come from?" Smooth inquired.

"One of your clients from Little Haiti. Shit crazy! Then Guru's girl pulled a set-it-off last night. She was killed by the police," Sue Rabbit explained.

"Damn, man! What the fuck is going on, bro?"

"Too much too fast, and too young, bro! We've made a killing. When you come out of that shit, let's just invest in some legitimate businesses. Feel me?" Sue Rabbit said to Smooth.

"Listen, Sue Rabbit. Guru's dead. Just as if it were you, my nigga, I wouldn't sleep until that wetback is in his grave," Smooth said.

"I feel that, bro!"

"You have sixty seconds remaining," the automated voice interrupted.

"Smooth! We gonna handle this shit. Just think about what I told you, bro."

"Thank you for using GTL," the automated voice said.

Damn it! I can't believe this! Smooth thought as he slammed the phone down loudly on the hook.

When Smooth turned around and walked toward his cell, an angry Haitian man named Lee stepped in front of him and looked Smooth in his eyes.

"Damn, bro. People do sleep in here in the mornings. You have no respect at all!" Lee said to Smooth.

"Man, you got a problem with it?"

Before Smooth could get the next words out of his mouth, Lee stole on him with a nimble three-piece. The impact knocked Smooth to the ground, extremely dazed. Lee was about to follow up and pound him some more until he saw the blood gushing from Smooth's nose and mouth. Lee looked at his hand and saw that his knuckles were split open.

"Shit!" Lee exclaimed while holding his hand. "I hope you not sick, muthafucka!"

As Lee strutted off, he thought he had gotten away with the fight until he saw the COs run into the dorm.

"Lee! Come here, boy. We caught that!" a sergeant named Ray said while holding his Taser aimed at Lee's chest with a red beam.

"Coward muthafucka! You stole me, nigga!" Smooth shouted as the other COs walked him from the dorm to medical to get treated. Lee surrendered and was cuffed, and then he was escorted to isolation.

In medical, Smooth was immediately treated for a broken nose and a badly busted lip, which was stitched up by a nurse for him. He then had to take a mandatory HIV test to make sure Lee wasn't infected with the virus. Until the test came back, Smooth was being locked down in the medical infirmary.

There is no way I'ma see Meka today, Smooth thought as he lay in the infirmary bed while holding an ice pack to his swollen lips.

All that was on his mind were the results of the HIV test.

* * *

China awoke around noon to dog breath from Zorro licking her face.

"Oh my gosh! Zorro, damn! Can a bitch get some decent rest?" China exclaimed as she threw a pillow at the dog's face and emerged from bed naked.

As she walked to the bathroom, she grabbed her iPhone and then locked Zorro outside the bathroom so she could take a piss in peace. As she relieved herself, she saw missed calls from Smooth, Sue Rabbit, and Spencer. She couldn't return Smooth's call, as much as she wanted to, so she called the next person she would rather hear in her ear.

Spencer's phone rang once before he answered. "Hello, sunshine!"

"How'd you know I was asleep? Maybe I was just busy, Mr. Know-It-All!" China said to Spencer.

"I know you were asleep because your nanny informed me. By the way, I brought you over some lunch. Thought you'd love to wake up to the best Italian food in Miami," Spencer said.

China smiled, loving that Spencer was such a gentleman.

"Thanks, Spencer. So what did you want?" China asked.

"I thought you were busy for the morning. Why'd you call at 9:00 a.m.?"

"Shit, China! How long does it take to cut a man's heart out?"

"Really?" China asked curiously.

"Hell yeah! I'll text it to you."

"No, Spencer, I believe you. Now what did you want?" China asked as she stood and flushed the toilet.

When she looked in the mirror, she realized that her nipples were erect.

Damn! What is this man doing to me?

"Did you hear about Guru's girlfriend?"

"No, what's wrong with her?" China asked.

"She walked into a bar and killed the bartender. She then ran outside and got herself killed by Metro-Dade police."

"Damn! That's terrible!"

"Tell me about it. She went out like a soldier, right?" Spencer asked in his white boy act.

It was amusing and caused China to burst into laughter.

"Boy, you are so crazy! Thanks for the news. I'll call you later when I get done handling my business today."

"Be careful, China," Spencer said.

"I will. Thanks," China said as she hung up.

She looked at herself in the mirror and caressed her nipples. "Damn! I have to get a grip on myself," she said as she hopped into the shower, where she again masturbated while thinking about Smooth.

"Damn! I hate to break the news to him about Guru," China said aloud while drying herself off.

After putting on some tights and a sports bra, China walked downstairs and found her nanny feeding Lucky.

"How is he?" she asked.

"He's pulling through. Yesterday was scary. He caught a fever, but it came down after a couple hours."

"Why didn't you call me, Amber?" China snapped.

"I'm so sorry, China. I thought I had everything under control, so there was no need to disturb you," Amber explained.

"Listen, Amber. If you see anything out of the normal, I don't care. Call me, okay?"

"Yes, ma'am. I will."

Amber was a twenty-four-year-old nanny who China had hired after finding her in an ad in the newspaper.

"Other than his fever, was there anything else?"

"No, ma'am," Amber replied, pulling the bottle out of Lucky's mouth.

China stared down at Lucky, who was badly shaking. "I swear I want to kill his mother!"

"The way she did this to him, she deserves it, China. But let God deal with her," Amber advised China.

"Thanks, Amber. But I'd never harm a soul in my life," China lied, hoping to sound innocent as an angel.

She didn't need a stranger knowing how cold her blood was.

"Umm, your friend dropped you off something to eat. It's in the oven. When I heard you in the shower, I started to warm it up for you."

"Thanks so much, Amber. I gotta add on to your salary for being so kind."

"It's okay, China. I just thought I'd help you out a little since you had a long night," Amber replied.

"Yes, tell me about it. It was a long night!" China said as she left Amber in the living room and strutted into the kitchen.

The redolence of fried chicken made her mouth water and her stomach turn.

Damn, I'm hungry! China thought as she opened the oven and found a hefty plate of soul food.

China grabbed the plate and sat down at the kitchen table, where she stuffed her face with the special from Roxy's.

Damn sis! You're about to be outdoing Kentucky Fried Chicken if you keep making this bomb-ass chicken! she thought.

China laughed when she remembered Spencer telling her that it was Italian food.

Now he knows this ain't no damn Italian food! China thought.

* * *

Meka was very upset when the receptionist informed her that Smooth couldn't receive any visitors due to his recent placement in the infirmary. She gave the receptionist a hard time, not believing what came out of her mouth. The receptionist was a woman that Meka knew resented her for fucking her husband years back. Meka threw her speculations in the receptionist's face and even called her out to the parking lot. It wasn't until Sgt. Ray came to calm down Meka and tell her that Smooth was indeed in the infirmary that she finally let it go.

He was involved in a damn fight after I told him not to do nothing stupid! Meka thought while driving through traffic.

She never noticed the black SUV trailing her when she came to a red light.

"That nigga told me that he wasn't gonna do nothing stupid. He even promised me. A nigga's word ain't worth shit!" Meka said as she accelerated through the green light.

When she passed by a McDonald's, she spotted Ham eating a cheeseburger while walking to his badly conditioned Chevy.

"Fuckin' loser!" she exclaimed, wishing that she could take Ham out right where he was standing.

Meka made a left onto a remote road that led to the hood.

"You're the reason why Smooth is sitting in jail now, you fucking coward!"

Crash!

"What the fuck!" Meka exclaimed when the SUV rammed into the back of her new Lexus.

Meka quickly braked and then unfastened her seatbelt after throwing the Lexus in park.

"I know this muthafucka ain't just run into my shit!" Meka exclaimed as she stepped out of her Lexus.

The driver's side door of the SUV was open, but the driver was still sitting in the front seat, which made Meka grow angrier. As she began walking over to the driver, the driver put the SUV in reverse.

"Oh no! You're not running bitch!" Meka said.

But she stopped short when she saw the gun come out of the window. She quickly turned on her heels and ran.

Boom! Boom! Boom! Boom!

Tic squeezed the trigger, nailing Meka and dropping her to her death.

He pulled up alongside her and then hopped out of the SUV. Tic walked up on Meka's lifeless body and emptied the clip into her.

"What a beautiful bitch to die on a beautiful day!" Tic said as he walked back to his SUV, hopped inside, and left the scene without any witnesses spotting him on the remote road.

When Tic made it back to his motel, he pulled out his iPhone and called his boss.

"Hello."

"The job is done, boss," Tic said.

"Good job. Lay down until I arrive on Sunday," Spencer said as he hung up the phone.

"I got you, boss," Tic replied as he exited the SUV and walked into his motel room.

* * *

"Mr. Johnson! I'm Nurse Sandra from the Martin County Health Department. And when my office is called, we come out and retest your first results. Well, we tested yours again, sir, and we got the same results."

"It can't be good if you're retesting them, ma'am. So, please, let's skip all this protocol shit," Smooth said to the elderly nurse.

"Son, my job is to tell you that you are HIV positive, and if you know anyone you've put at risk, please contact them and inform them to get tested. We will start you on medications today, but when you get out, you have to report to a doctor yourself to continue the medications," the nurse said to Smooth, whose mind was not on her but on the two females who could have given him the deadly virus—Meka and Jane.

But both women looked too healthy to be infected with HIV, he thought.

Smooth was so hurt by the news that he didn't realize he was crying.

"Baby, you gotta warn your partner," Nurse Sandra expressed.

Yeah, I know, but do I have the heart to tell her? Smooth thought.

20

ROXY KNEW THAT Sue Rabbit was going through a tough time grieving the death of Guru. So she took off and let Nicole, her assistant manager, run the restaurant. She wanted to be by Sue Rabbit's side like a real woman was supposed to do when her man was down.

They had just finished making love for the umpteenth time that day, and Roxy felt that it was time to inform Sue of the wonderful news that she had been keeping to herself for a month straight. Roxy climbed on top of Sue Rabbit and straddled him while looking into his eyes. She kissed him and then smiled at him. He knew the look well that something was on her mind.

"What's the grin for?" Sue Rabbit asked.

"Trayvon, how much do you love me?"

"I love you more than words could explain, Roxy," Sue said, choking back tears.

"Don't worry, baby. Let them fall," Roxy said to him while he was wiping his tears away.

"I know you love me, Trayvon. Now it's time to love us," Roxy said.

"I do love us, baby," Sue Rabbit replied.

"No, baby. Not me and you. I want you to love us!" Roxy said as she grabbed Sue Rabbit's hand and placed it on her stomach. "We've made a creation, and I want us to be one big happy family. This is just number one."

"Are you serious, baby?" Sue Rabbit asked excitedly as he tightly hugged Roxy.

"Yes, baby. I'm serious," Roxy said as she kissed him repeatedly.

Sue Rabbit flipped Roxy onto her back and slowly entered her wet pussy.

"Mmm!" Roxy moaned out, wrapping her legs around Sue Rabbit's back. "I love you, Trayvon," she exclaimed as Sue Rabbit thrust in and out of her love box.

"I love you too, baby. I want a baby boy."

"No, I want a girl!" Roxy exclaimed.

"No, a boy!" Sue Rabbit said as he plunged deeper inside. "Uhhh shit!"

"A boy, I say!"

"No, a girl!" Roxy moaned.

"Twins!"

"Yes, baby! Twins!" Roxy agreed.

"I love you, baby," Sue Rabbit whispered into Roxy's ear as he started sucking on her ear and neck.

"Mmmmm! I love you too, daddy!" Roxy purred.

Damn! I'm about to be a father. Smooth, like it or not, homie, I got to give up the game, Sue Rabbit thought while making love to Roxy.

Together, Sue and Roxy came to their climax and held each other until their climax subsided.

"Give me a minute!" Sue Rabbit said.

Sue Rabbit got out of the bed naked as Roxy watched him walk to the closet. She watched him dig into the pocket of a pair of jeans that were hanging on a cloth hanger on the rack. He returned to bed holding a black velvet box.

"Baby! I know I've told you that I'm leaving this game alone, and I mean it. From seeing my homie get killed to Smooth being set up, that's all the game has to offer. It takes the smart, wise, prudent—all of the above—to get you and then get out. I dropped a whole football team of women for you. Roxy, a man like me who could drop the game for a better life deserves a wife. And I'm asking you, Roxy Morrine Preston, to be my wife!"

"Oh my gosh!" Roxy exclaimed, covering her mouth with both hands trembling when Sue Rabbit showed her the big diamond and platinum ring.

The ring has to be worth a quarter million dollars! If not, then close to it! Roxy thought, completely awestruck.

"Will you marry me, Roxy?"

"Yes, Trayvon!" Roxy choked on her tears. "I will marry you."

Sue Rabbit removed the ring from the box, grabbed her trembling hand, and slid the ring onto her finger.

"I love you, woman, and I refuse to let these streets take me from you," Sue Rabbit professed as he kissed her hand like a king would to his queen.

"I love you too," Roxy replied with so much emotion in her voice.

* * *

When Agent Jones got the urgent call to report to the Metro-Dade County Jail to meet with an inmate who had information but wished to remain anonymous, she hurried and got over to the jail. She had no idea who the inmate was or what information he was willing to give up.

When she entered the investigation unit of the jail, she met with Captain Baldwin, who she had known for many years. He thought she was the strongest black woman he had ever met. He was a white man in his mid-fifties, who stood six four and weighed 205 pounds, and he had a thing for black women.

"Nice day, Jones," Captain Baldwin said as he escorted her down the hallway that led to the interview room, where the inmate sat at the table with his head down.

"He wrote an inmate request form and asked to speak with a captain. I came to investigate the problem, and he asked for you," Captain Baldwin briefed Jones outside the interview room.

When Agent Jones took a look inside at the inmate, who now had his head up, she smiled after identifying him.

The big ones always break! Agent Jones thought.

"Thanks, Baldwin. I really appreciate you getting in contact with me," Agent Jones said with a smile on her face.

"You're always welcome, Jones. I'll be close by in the booth, recording for you," Baldwin said as he walked off.

When Agent Jones looked back into the interview room, the inmate's head was back down in his hands on the table. Once she entered the room, the inmate looked up, and Jones could see his eyes, bloodshot from crying. She was accustomed to seeing inmates break, so it didn't bother her to see someone crying.

"Mr. Corey Nelson. I never thought that it would be you in a million years," Jones spoke as she took a seat at the table.

"Yeah, well it's true!"

"Wait a minute! Before I speak with you, I have to inform you of your constitutional rights," Jones said as she read him his Miranda rights.

When she was done, she asked him if he understood his rights, and he agreed that he did. It was a protocol that had to be followed for evidence to stick against a witness or suspect in court.

"So tell me, Nelson, what are we here for?" Agent Jones asked him.

"I know who Smooth is," Big Mitch informed Jones.

It took all the strength and training techniques she'd learned for Jones to bridle her excitement.

"So you personally know who Smooth is?" Jones asked while jotting down information on her yellow notepad.

"Yeah, I know that pussy muthafucka!" Big Mitch said, with so much hatred in his voice. "His name is Donavan Johnson."

After Big Mitch learned that China and Sue Rabbit had slumped all his workers, he wanted revenge. Five of the workers were Big Mitch's cousins, and now he wanted Smooth and everyone involved to pay for it.

"So how are you acquainted with Donavan, Nelson?" Agent Jones began.

"Listen, lady! Before I tell you anything else, I want to get this clear. I'm not giving this information for nothing. I need to walk them streets again. I'm thirty-seven and got a fifteen-year-old daughter who needs me."

"And I understand that, Nelson. You know if my office can help you, then we will," Jones told him as he began to chuckle.

"See, woman, I don't know shit about your office. I never dealt with you people. Let's not forget that you people sent me to prison at eighteen years old. We have never gotten along!" he replied.

"Okay, that's in the past. What are you looking for now?"

"I'm looking to get the fuck out of here for giving y'all who you've been looking for. I'm not like everyone else. Like I said, I know the boss personally," Big Mitch informed.

"Do you know where we can find him?" Jones asked.

"Of course I know where to find him. But like I said, until we come to an agreement, I don't know who the fuck y'all talking about," Big Mitch said as he crossed his arms.

He knew what he was doing was a coward move that could get him killed, but he had to free himself and get to Smooth's bitch. Money was another name on his list who he wanted to get. He was told by one of Sue Rabbit's lieutenants that Money helped set up the slaughter trap where his cousins were killed.

"Mr. Nelson, could you give me a day to get with my superiors to discuss a deal?" Agent Jones asked.

"Take a week if you want. Just remember that I'm not disclosing his location until y'all talking right," Big Mitch reiterated.

"Okay, Mr. Nelson. I will be in contact with you in a day or so. Pretty much, you'll get this deal once I voice it. Just don't make me look bad," Agent Jones said as she gathered her things to leave.

"Work your magic, and I'll do my part," Big Mitch told her as she made it to the door.

"Okay, Nelson. Like I said, give me a day or so," Jones said as she departed from the room with a smile on her face.

Agent Jones walked into the booth where Captain Baldwin was awaiting her with three of Donavan Johnson's juvenile mug shots.

"Recognize your man?" Captain Baldwin asked Jones, who immediately laid eyes on the man called Smooth, who everyone knew to be the boss.

"Yeah, that's him. Is there an address?"

"His last address was a foster home, but that was years ago."

"I see you still have your touch, Captain Baldwin."

"Agent Jones, I've been in this field just as long as you have. Catching criminals will never get old for me. No matter where I'm at."

"Thanks. Well, I have to go see what deal I can bring Mr. Nelson."

"Make sure you exhaust all of your resources first. He slipped up when he gave you his name, and I think he knows that," Baldwin said.

"Let's pray that he did slip up. You know what I mean?"

"Exactly!" Captain Baldwin replied.

* * *

The news of Meka's death had Ham paranoid. It seemed that everybody who was close to him was falling dead. They were all murdered, and something in his gut told him that the man suspected of killing Banga had something to do with killing Meka. Ham just knew that he was next on the list to die.

But who killed Tina and took our baby? Ham wanted to know.

He was stuck in his bedroom smoking his crack, and all the lights were out. He was waiting for his turn to die. If it was not tonight, Ham thought he'd have a chance to go get his enemy and supplier.

Knock! Knock! Knock!

"Who's there?" Ham shouted as he grabbed his Glock .40 at the sound of knocking.

Ham stood near the door of his bedroom and walked to the front door with his gun in his hand. Without checking the peephole, Ham opened the door and regretted it the moment he saw his visitor. Ham put his hand behind his back to hide the gun.

"Hamilton, you smell like a kilo of fucking crack, son. Do we need to place you in rehab, or are you just stressing?" Sgt. Running Man said to Ham, whose eyes were bloodshot red.

"I'm okay, man. Someone killed my cousin," Ham said.

"That's exactly why I'm here to talk with you about it, Hamilton. Do you know who could have done this to her?" Running Man asked.

"I have no clue, sir."

"What about Tina Scott? Can you tell her to come to the door?" the sergeant said.

Ham's eyes shot wide open from panic and fear of the sergeant discovering Tina's remains in the freezer.

"Is something wrong?" Running Man asked Ham, who looked like he had just seen a ghost.

"Tina . . . Tina . . . Tina?" Ham stuttered. "She's not home."

"What? Is she somewhere inside, just as high as you are?"

"No! She's not here, Sergeant," Ham said, trying to straighten up.

"Back up, Hamilton," Sgt. Running Man ordered, sensing that Ham was lying to him.

The sergeant artistically removed his Glock .21 and flashlight and aimed it at Ham's chest.

"I'ma tell you one more time, Hamilton! Back the fuck up before I blow your damn head off!"

"Sergeant, I don't want no problems! I have my gun in my hand, sir. Please don't shoot me," Ham begged.

"Drop the gun asshole!"

Ham did as he was ordered and then put his hands in the air.

"Sergeant, I don't want no problems! Tina's not here with me no more," Ham informed Running Man.

"Boy, if you didn't have a job to do, I would have had your ass in a box somewhere!" the sergeant told him.

"I know, sir. I'm just trying to be in my own world," Ham said.

Sgt. Running Man reached down and picked up Ham's gun. He released the clip and let it fall to the floor, and then he tossed the gun across the living room floor. He then shined his light into the dark kitchen, which made Ham even more nervous. The sergeant looked around the kitchen and then took a tour of the apartment, with Ham on his heels. Like Ham had told him, Tina was nowhere to be found.

The bitch isn't here for real, Sgt. Running Man thought.

"Get this place cleaned up, Hamilton! When your kid comes, DES could take him away. You don't want that to happen," Sgt. Running Man told Ham as he walked toward the front door to make his exit.

"I will, sir. Today I will do it," Ham replied, happy to see Sgt. Running Man leaving.

"And do me a favor. Don't let me catch you high again, and get rid of that gun. I need you to be clean for court. Don't make me look bad, or I'll have you rotting in prison," the sergeant promised.

"I got you, sir. I will straighten up!"

"See you around, Hamilton," Sgt. Running Man said as he walked out to his unmarked SUV, never noticing the black SUV parked a couple apartments down and the man watching his every move.

"Snitching-ass nigga!" Tic said as he pulled off, after Sgt. Running Man drove out of the apartment complex.

* * *

It was bothering China that she hadn't heard from Smooth all day. She had missed his calls in the morning, and she had been waiting for a call ever since. Once ten o'clock came around, she knew that the inmates would be locking down. At twelve o'clock, China waited for Spencer to arrive, and he showed up one minute later. She then hopped inside the stolen Dodge Ram pickup truck with him.

It was forty-five minutes later when Spencer pulled up to the trap house on 12th Street in Little Haiti. The house was active, and a television could be heard and seen illuminating the living room.

"Give me ten minutes once I'm inside," China said to Spencer.

"Okay."

China pulled down her mini jersey dress, grabbed her Prada purse, and then exited the truck. China walked up to the house in which she knew only four men were inside. Any more than that would be unexpected.

China climbed the steps and then listened attentively for any signs of surprises. She had purposely approached the Jamaican named JoJo earlier and gotten him to agree to a late-night visit, but only if the cash was right. She specifically told him that she wanted a four-man setup for $3,200. The deal was sealed.

China knocked on the door and waited for someone to answer. When the door opened, she saw that it was JoJo, who was smoking a phat kush blunt.

"I've been waiting on you, mami!" JoJo said as he blew smoke in China's face.

"I'm sure you have. Can I come in?"

"Come on, beautiful. The others are asleep. How about me and you go first?"

"That's not part of the deal. And if that's the case, I'll go and give your money back. I know what I came here for. There's plenty of niggas who know how to pay for the pussy," China said with an attitude.

"Feisty mami. Just how me like it!" JoJo said as he ran his hands down China's hips and ass.

"Come upstairs," JoJo said and then led the way.

When they got upstairs, JoJo led China to a master bedroom and let her get comfortable.

"Anything to drink?"

"Yeah. Jamaican nut all down my throat!" China replied.

"Damn, mami! Let me get the rest!" JoJo said as he walked out of the room.

When he arrived with the rest of his team, the room was completely dark.

"She likes the kinky shit, mon!" one of them said.

JoJo tried to flick on the light in the room but got no illumination, because China had removed the light bulb. The room was too dark for any of them to see China aiming her two Glock .40s at them.

"You four snitched on Stone, man?" China shouted.

"This bitch is crazy, mon!"

Boom! Boom! Boom! Boom!

China squeezed the trigger of both Glocks, hitting the four Jamaicans in their torsos and faces. JoJo was lucky to escape the face shots and was still breathing when China walked up on him.

"Stone told me to tell you, suck his dick and welcome to hell!" China said to JoJo as she squeezed off two shots to his face.

China ran back into the room and grabbed her purse off the bed. She then ran downstairs, leaving the chilling scene behind her.

Stone's worries are now taken care of, China thought as she hopped back inside the Dodge Ram.

"That's good timing," Spencer complimented China.

"What if I was a minute later?" she asked.

"Then I would have come to get the Jamaican men off of you," Spencer replied.

"That's why I like you, Spencer. I can really count on you."

"The same here," Spencer responded sincerely.

They rode to China's house in silence. China realized that Spencer was like her in a lot of ways. After a murder, silence was needed to replay every detail. It was the fun part to China and Spencer. If not replaying all the details, they were planning their next kill. When Spencer made it to the house, China felt the need to offer him a drink.

"Do you want to come inside for a drink?"

"Nah, sorry. I gotta get rid of this truck," Spencer said.

"I understand," China replied as she exited the truck and headed inside.

21

IT SEEMED LIKE the moment her head hit the pillow, it was dawn. Hearing her iPhone ring at 8:00 a.m., she knew it was no one other than Smooth. She answered, eager to hear his voice.

"Hello."

"This is a collect call from the Martin County Jail."

China pressed 0 to bypass the prompts and accept his call.

"Smooth?"

"What's good, baby?" Smooth's voice said sadly.

He knows about Guru, China concluded. "Are you okay, baby?"

"Yeah, I'm cool."

"So I'm guessing you've heard about Guru."

"Yeah, and I still can't believe that he's gone, China," Smooth said. "Then Landi completely lost it."

"No one can believe it, baby. But we know what is possible out here in these streets," China reminded Smooth.

"So, when will I see you?" Smooth asked.

China didn't want to tell him over the phone that she would be in Martin County on Sunday, plus she had plans to go see Jefe and Jenny.

"I'ma try to slide through Monday sometime, baby," she said.

"Okay, I'll be waiting."

"Smooth, can I ask you a question, and I want an honest answer from you."

"What is it, baby?" Smooth replied, expecting China to drop another bombshell in his life.

He was HIV positive, and he had just found out on the local news that Meka, the woman who had probably given him the virus, was killed by an unknown assassin.

"Smooth, when you was out in this world and I was incarcerated, you were fucking any bitch that opened her legs."

There it goes! he thought.

"And I respected the game, right?" China reminded him.

"Yes, you did, China. Where is this going?" Smooth asked.

"So what if I meet someone that I just want to have fun with?" China asked, getting a line of silence in response.

She wants to mingle, Smooth thought.

"China, if you want to have fun, go ahead. I can't get mad at you. I can only advise you to use protection," Smooth said, wanting to inform her of his new status.

But he couldn't bring himself to do it as much as he couldn't see China with another man. He knew that he would be being selfish if he snapped on her about something he was doing while she was in prison.

"Baby, I love you so much. You're too real. You've just agreed to let me mingle out of respect. Why is it so easy?"

"Because I know no matter who comes into your life, it's only for the moment. But we're forever!" Smooth replied, causing China to tear up.

"Baby, you need to come home," China choked up on the tears she could no longer control. "I miss you so much."

"I'm coming, baby. Just give the process time to develop, and make sure that you guys handle business," Smooth said.

"So tell me. Who's the lucky guy?" Smooth asked.

"There's no lucky man, Smooth. Just you and me," China replied, drying her eyes.

"No woman?"

"Not if she's not Jenny," China informed Smooth.

Wow! So she's just testing me to see what a nigga's answer would be, Smooth considered.

"Baby, we stand together in loyalty, and I never forgot that. Yeah, my dick may have gotten tender, but no woman has had enough pussy power to make me leave my wifey!" Smooth informed China.

"Baby, can I ask you a question?"

"What's up, China?"

"Did you and Amanda have anything going on other than business?"

Damn! I can't lie to her. It'd be foolish, especially if she has some kind of proof, Smooth thought.

"Yes, China," Smooth sighed. "We were friends with—"

"You have sixty seconds left," the automated voice announced.

"So that night you called me her name. You were thinking of her, huh?" China asked with an attitude.

Smooth did not want the call to end this way.

"Baby, listen. I love you. No woman has ever made me change or hurt."

"Thank you for using GTL," the automated voice said.

"I knew you two were fucking around, Smooth! Thank you for being honest," China said as she then called Sue Rabbit, who picked up on the second ring.

"What's up, China?" Sue Rabbit answered.

"How much do you need? I'm taking a trip in two days," China informed Sue Rabbit.

"We need three hundred of them. I want to make this the last trip until Smooth touches down."

"Okay, that sounds smart," China agreed. "Hey, let me ask you a question."

"What's up, China?"

"Where can I find Amanda?"

"No one knows where's she's disappeared to, and I find it fishy, especially when she's suspect."

"Why do you say she's suspect?" China inquired.

"She was with Smooth when he got knocked off. She walks in the store, and bam, feds swarm Smooth," Sue Rabbit explained, filling China's ears with new devastating news.

He took that bitch to New York with him! she concluded.

"China, I wouldn't be surprised if she has a part in setting him up. I'm judging this by her sudden disappearance, feel me?" Sue Rabbit said to her.

"So she's AWOL?" China asked.

"AWOL. Completely off the map," Sue Rabbit replied.

"Yeah, that does look fishy. Well, get back with me if you do see her," China informed Sue.

"I will, sis!"

"Thanks! Where's Roxy?"

"She went over to GaGa's to drop her off a plate of breakfast."

"Okay, Sue Rabbit. Stay safe!" China said as she hung up the phone.

This nigga took this bitch to New York with him. That's why he avoided all my calls that weekend. Why do I even accept this shit, Smooth? China asked herself.

Before the tears could fall, she caught them and wiped them away with her hands.

"I'm done crying, Smooth. Two can play that game," China said as she walked downstairs where she found Amber feeding a bottle to Lucky.

"Good morning, China."

"Good morning to you too, Amber. How is he?" China asked.

"He's having fun today," Amber said as she pulled the bottle from Lucky's mouth and then picked him up to burp him.

"I'll do it. Let me see him," China asked.

"Okay," Amber said as she handed him over to China.

When China put him in her arms and began to burp him, she noticed the increased weight that he had put on.

"He's definitely put on some pounds," China said as she burped Lucky while he still badly shook.

"Yeah, he has! He's growing stronger every day," Amber informed China.

"Thank you for all your help, Amber. I wouldn't know what to do without your help," China admitted.

"I'm glad to be able to help you, China. I want you to take a look at his belly cord. It's getting infected."

"Really?" China exclaimed in panic.

She was worried about the way she cut the cord. When she lay the baby down on the sofa and checked his navel, she laughed. Amber became a little perplexed as China continued to laugh.

"Amber, you almost scared me. There's nothing to worry about. He just has a big-ass belly button," China said.

"So he's alright?"

"Yes, Amber. He's fine," China reassured her as she handed him back to her.

"I have to run a couple errands, but I'll be back before ten o'clock tonight."

"Take your time, China. I'm okay. I love this place," Amber said.

"Okay, see you later then," China said as she walked back upstairs.

China took a shower and then put on a pair of skintight H&M jeans. While she was combing her hair, her phone rang. When she checked to see the caller, it was Smooth. Not wanting to hear shit from him, she answered and refused the call so he would get the message.

"I have no time for games and to waste my life missing out!" China said as she resumed combing out her hair.

* * *

"Damn it!" Smooth exclaimed after hearing China refuse his call.

He knew China was upset about Amanda.

So why ask a nigga for the truth if you can't handle it? he thought as he tried calling her back again but got no answer.

He had no female companion to turn to. Meka was dead, Amanda was AWOL, and now China was upset about him keeping it real with her. He thought about what China asked him about mingling.

She can't deal with being alone, just as much as I couldn't when she went to prison. How can I get mad and be selfish? he thought as he walked back to his cell.

Rosco and Baby Dread were already playing chess. To clear his mind, he leaned on the wall and watched the two contenders go at it, move after move, five minutes ahead of each other.

Just like I failed to do. If I was playing five moves ahead of the game, I wouldn't be HIV positive, Smooth thought regretfully.

He had a hard time trying to figure out if it was Jane or Meka who could have given him the virus. He even thought that Amanda herself could have given it to him and pretended to be infected by him first. He was confused and didn't know how to tell China. He was afraid of her reaction and afraid that he would lose her. He knew that he couldn't infect her by being selfish.

She just doesn't deserve it, he thought.

"Check!" Baby Dread shouted, putting Rosco in check.

Rosco moved his king, and Baby Dread pushed his queen up for another check.

"Check!" Rosco moved his king out of check again, and Smooth immediately saw the checkmate move, but Baby Dread himself didn't. He moved too fast and moved the wrong piece. His queen allowed Rosco to swindle out.

"Rosco makes all his foes slip," Rosco said as he showed Baby Dread his mistake.

"Moving this knight for checkmate would have been a game for you," Rosco said before he made a power move that put him in good position.

Is that what happened to me? I saw the best move but took the wrong one? Smooth asked himself. *I gotta keep it real with China. I fucked up. I can't ruin her life for my mistake.*

He loved China too much to ruin her life. She had to know that her childhood sweetheart was now HIV positive.

* * *

When China pulled up to Smooth's apartment complex, she saw that Sue Rabbit was at the trap apartment.

He's probably cooking up the last of his product, China thought as she parked next to his Range Rover.

She was coming to collect Jane's rent money before she drove over to GaGa's to eat lunch with her. Before she walked over to Jane's, she decided to stop in and check up on Sue

Rabbit. She got out of her Benz and walked up to his door. Before she could knock, the door opened, and she saw that Sue was on the phone. He waved her in and then walked back into the kitchen. The smell of cocaine being cooked lingered strongly in the air.

I can't stay in this bitch too long, China thought as she closed the front door and locked it.

"Yeah! Ummm, we still gonna do that, bro, like I said? Just give me a couple hours," Sue Rabbit said to the party on the phone. "Okay, hit me in one hour."

When China looked in the kitchen, she saw an old-school woman at the stove cooking up the cocaine.

Amanda is definitely not cooking. That's why I came in here, huh? China thought, catching her curiosity.

"What's up, China?" Sue Rabbit asked, after hanging up the phone with his client.

"Just dropping by to pick up rent money from next door. I didn't know that you would be over here," China replied.

"Yeah, trying to make room. Like I said, I want this to be the last run until Smooth comes home. This shit is getting old, and we have money to just fall back on."

Damn! Why can't Smooth be here to hear this shit? If yo' homeboy could back out of the game, then you could too! China deliberated.

"Sue Rabbit, I agree with you. I've been telling Smooth that since before he ended up behind bars," China informed Sue while looking at the lady cooking at the stove. "She looks like she knows what she's doing."

"That's Cookie, but she likes to be called Auntie. She indeed knows what she's doing."

"Well, I'm not staying long. I don't want any secondhand smoke off of crack," China said as she walked back toward the front door with Sue Rabbit.

Sue Rabbit badly wanted to share the good news of being a father and husband to her sister, but he decided to let Roxy tell her.

"Well, I'll see you later," Sue said to China, walking her out the door.

"Okay, Sue Rabbit. Be careful."

"Always."

China left her car parked next to the Range Rover and walked the short distance to Jane's apartment. When she got to her door, she knocked twice.

"I'm coming," Jane shouted.

"Girl, hurry up! It's hot as hell out here!" China shouted back.

When the door came open, China saw that Jane was wrapped in a towel and appeared to be fresh out of the shower. *Damn, this bitch is gorgeous!* China thought.

"Bitch, don't look at me like that. I'm strictly dickly. Ain't no woman munching on this carpet!" Jane said as she walked inside, allowing China to follow her.

"Make yourself at home while I put on some clothes," Jane told her.

Once China stepped into the air-conditioned apartment, she walked into the kitchen. She was extremely thirsty and in need of a glass of water. China set down her purse on the table and raided the fridge. She grabbed a jug of punch and found a clean glass. After pouring herself a glass, she returned the jug back into the fridge and sat at the kitchen table. Just as she took a sip, she spit all the juice out of her mouth onto the floor when her eye caught sight of Jane's stack of mail on her table.

What the fuck! China said to herself as she grabbed the first letter off the stack with trembling hands.

"Donavan Johnson," China read the name off the envelope.

When she looked at the sender's address, she had no doubt that she was staring at her man's letter addressed to Jane. China tore open the envelope and saw by the date that it was an old letter which Jane had not yet opened.

China read, "What's good, Ms. Pretty Pussy. I know that you know where I am. A nigga be thinking about you every night. I miss how you put that pussy down on a nigga, and how that ass jiggled when I slapped it. How about sending me some pictures in some nice bikini, boo? I need you to keep my dick hard until I get back. Sincerely, Smooth."

China couldn't believe what she had just read. The pain had numbed her body so quickly that she didn't even feel the tears cascading down her face as she stood and dug into her purse for her Glock .40. When she grabbed her Glock, she cocked it back and then walked toward Jane's bedroom with the letter in her hand. When she entered the bedroom, she caught Jane applying cocoa butter lotion to her legs while sitting on the edge of the bed. Jane looked up and saw a disturbed China with a gun in her hand and a letter in the other. She became frightened.

"What's wrong, China?"

"I'ma ask you one time, Jane. How can you explain fucking my man behind my back?"

Oh shit! Jane thought, realizing that China had found the letter that Smooth wrote her that she had never opened.

"China, I can explain!"

"I'm waiting, Jane," China said as she aimed her Glock at her.

Jane laughed and then swiped her curly hair out of her face.

"I'm glad you think it's funny, bitch!" China said.

"China, your man came on to me. I pushed him away. Yeah, the dick was good, but it wasn't nothing to keep around," Jane explained.

"How could you cross me, Jane? I gave you a job and a place to stay. I thought you were my friend!" China cried out to her.

"I'm sorry, China."

Boom!

China squeezed the trigger and shot Jane between her breasts. Jane's eyes expanded, and her mouth shot wide open.

"You betrayed me, bitch!" China said.

"Bitch. I been dead!"

Boom! Boom! Boom!

China pulled the trigger and emptied the whole clip into Jane.

"I know, bitch! Dead bitch walking, huh? You knew China was going to catch your ass?" China said, not realizing what Jane was actually telling her.

China left the apartment without anyone seeing her or hearing the shots. When she got into her Benz and pulled off, she just knew that she was done with Smooth. He had crossed the line by fucking her friend, and had to pay for it just like she did.

I'ma kill him! China thought as she drove over to GaGa's house.

22

WHEN STONE SAW the news of the discovered murders in Little Haiti, it only took him one look to realize that he was staring at one of his trap houses.

"Four men found dead in a drug house" is what the Latina news reporter informed everyone watching the television.

When Stone saw the body bags being carried out, he smiled and thought about China.

Baby gal handle business like a soldier, Stone thought, with a smile on his face.

Stone was feeling like a million-dollar man again. Without JoJo and his other three workers, he had a chance to take his case to trial and win. Stone left the dayroom area and walked back into his cell, where he could be alone. Seeing that his reach was so far and unexpected gave him a new respect for China and Smooth.

"I gotta keep them both on my team when me get outta here and go back to Jamaica," Stone said to himself while looking in the mirror.

I wish I had China's number. I'd kiss thee gal through the phone, he thought.

Stone took off his tank top and started his daily workout. He got on the floor and did a rep of push-ups. Stone worked out every day after the last meal was wheeled into the dorm. He was doing another set when the dorm got dead quiet.

What the hell is going on now? Stone thought of the sudden silence.

He knew that when shit got quiet, there was something going on that wasn't supposed to be going on. When he looked up, he saw Captain Baldwin with four COs and two sergeants walking toward his cell.

Thought y'all would have come sooner, Stone thought as the entourage entered his cell.

"Mr. Stone Bolt, we need you to come with us. Cuff up, and let's take a walk," the captain said, with handcuffs in his hands.

"I got him, Captain," a sergeant said as he stepped forward and cuffed a not resistant Stone.

"Can someone inform me of what's going on?" Stone asked.

"I'm sure you're aware, Mr. Bolt. Everyone knows what's going on in Little Haiti. Do you have any information?" Captain Baldwin asked.

"So, I'ma need my lawyer right, mon?" Stone asked.

"Send him to the hole. Security threat to our facility," Baldwin ordered his COs and sergeants.

"Yes, sir," a sergeant replied as he walked Stone to isolation.

* * *

Agent Jones was pissed after learning that Stone Bolt immediately screamed for his lawyer. But despite Stone's uncooperative attitude, Jones had good news for Big Mitch. When she met him in the interrogation room, he was very attentive and eager to hear what she had to offer him. Without wasting any time, Agent Jones removed two documents from a folder and slid them across the table to Big Mitch.

"Can you read?"

"Do it look like I can't?" Big Mitch shot back, feeling offended.

"The best we can do is nine months, with a year probation

and a year of house arrest," Jones said. "It's better than life in prison, Nelson. Sign on the highlighted line."

"I told you I wanted to be free, and not set up to fall back in the system, lady," Big Mitch said.

"And I told you that this is the best my office could do, Nelson. Take it or leave it!" Agent Jones said.

Fuck! I don't want to be on house arrest. That's a straight up set up, Big Mitch thought.

He saw it more like a trap for his enemies to have easy access to catch him at home if the deal backfired.

"Nelson, this isn't something hard to think about. You're looking at life in prison. What's nine months followed by a year on house arrest?"

"How easy is it for my enemies to find me at home?"

"That's nothing to worry about. We will set you up in our protection program," Agent Jones informed Big Mitch.

"Now we're talking," Big Mitch said as he signed both documents without reading them.

"Now, give me Donavan Johnson's location," Agent Jones ordered.

"That's easy! Try looking at the Martin County Jail in Stuart, Florida. He's looking at a boatload of time," Big Mitch said as he winked at Agent Jones, who felt extremely stupid and cheated out of her own game.

She wasn't happy with the system one bit. When she first looked up his name, it should have shown that he was incarcerated. *So what the fuck is Martin County hiding?* Agent Jones thought.

"Thank you, Big Mitch."

"No! Thank you, Agent Jones," Big Mitch said with a smile.

When Agent Jones came into the booth with Captain Baldwin, she found him on the computer pulling up Donavan Johnson's file in Martin County.

"Bingo!" Captain Baldwin shouted, when he got a hit from the Martin County data. "Arrested by Martin County DEA after an informer revealed a trafficking drop. Suspect was found in possession of one hundred kilos of cocaine. He was positively identified by informer #12143CJr, whoever the hell that is!" Baldwin informed Jones, who was jotting down everything on her notepad.

"Looks like we're on our way to Martin County," Agent Jones said to the captain.

"Good luck, pit bull in a skirt!"

"Shut up! I hate it when you call me that!" Jones laughed.

"I think I'm the only one who can get away with it."

"You are, Captain!" Agent Jones assured him.

* * *

"I'd really like to thank you, Nurse Tara."

"You can just call me Tara, and like I told you, he will be okay. We will find a home for him," Tara said to China, who had just given Lucky away to be cared for and placed in a nice home.

After China explained to Spencer her desire to get rid of the baby, Spencer suggested that she let him help her. When Nurse Tara showed up at Spencer's luxurious beach house, China was surprised to see the nurse who had cared for her. She had no idea that Spencer and Tara were friends.

"Well, I guess we'll be on our way," Tara said while holding Lucky in a car seat.

China took one more look at the baby and got teary-eyed. She tried to control herself, but all she could think about was the loss of her own baby. She wanted to care for Lucky like he was hers, but she couldn't. She could only feel content knowing that she had saved Lucky from crib death or an overdose.

"Don't worry, China. He will be well taken care of," Tara reminded her. "See you two later," she said to China and Spencer, who were both sitting at his mini bar.

"Okay, Tara. Drive safe," Spencer said.

When Tara was gone, China sighed, wiped her face, and turned around, staring into Spencer's eyes.

"Do you really trust her not to go to the police?" China asked, immediately feeling stupid after the words left her mouth.

She knew that if Spencer didn't trust Tara, then he wouldn't have called her.

"Relax, China, and have a drink with me," Spencer said as he poured her a glass of Remy on the rocks.

"How come I gotta accept your offer when you always decline mine?" China asked.

"Because you're always offering me coffee and not a man's drink."

"I've always said to help yourself," China said, with her hands on her hips and a sexy pout on her face.

Despite her protest, China walked over to the bar and took the drink. As she took a sip, Spencer stared at her with lust in his eyes.

"Why are you looking at me like that?" China asked Spencer, who came closer to her.

He then took his hand and rubbed the scar on the bridge of China's nose and gently felt the scar on her lips. Before she could say anything, Spencer leaned into her and softly kissed her lips. China brought her hand to his face and caressed the smoothness of his baby face while looking him in his adorable eyes. China then leaned into Spencer and responded with a passionate kiss. She was amazed at how great a kisser he was. Spencer stood and picked China up off her feet and carried her to the living room. She kissed him the entire way. Spencer then laid China down on the sofa and tore off her blouse. In return, China tore off Spencer's dress shirt and wrapped her arms around his neck while he sucked on her erect nipples.

"Spencer!" China purred.

Spencer helped her out of her jeans and slid off her black thong. Neither of them could believe what was happening, but neither of them wanted to stop. Spencer stood up and took off his jeans. When China saw his fully erect cock, she was amazed at how nicely he was hung. His cock reminded her of a porn star's cock. She spread her legs and invited Spencer inside. When he slowly slid inside her tight pussy, she was gasping for air as she was all choked up on passion.

"Oh my gosh, Spencer! It feels so good!" China purred loudly as Spencer sank inside her love box as deep as he could.

China clawed at his back and bit down on his shoulder. The pain quickly subsided to pleasure. As Spencer slow-stroked her, China was enjoying giving herself to another man.

Smooth was the only man she had given herself to, and now it was over between them. China couldn't see herself forgiving him for his infidelity. He had fucked her friend, and she was now fucking his hit man. Spencer kissed her tears away and helped her get Smooth out of her system. He had no clue what she was going through, but he knew how to comfort her undisclosed pain.

"Spencer, I'm coming!" China purred loudly as she came to a stimulating orgasm.

He's definitely a winner. He made me come. This is no white boy, China thought as Spencer continued to thrust in and out of her love box.

They found themselves having sex until dawn approached. They then showered together and had sex again before China departed for home.

* * *

When China pulled up to her house, she met Roxy, who was sitting in her Lexus about to pull off. China realized that her iPhone was still turned off after her second round with Spencer. She wanted no interruptions to ruin her time with him. As China stepped out of the Benz wearing one of Spencer's T-shirts, Roxy was stepping out of her Lexus. She looked stressed and like she was crying.

"Roxy, are you okay?"

"Oh my gosh, China! You won't believe this, but someone killed Jane, and Tabby just found her this morning," Roxy informed China.

"Damn! That's crazy! I just saw her yesterday," China replied in feigned disbelief.

China was doing everything but crying. She wished she could tell Roxy everything, but she knew that her sister couldn't stomach the truth.

"Sue Rabbit said the same thing. We were worried about you, and Smooth has been trying to get in touch with you. I talked to him an hour ago when he called Sue's phone."

"Fuck Smooth, Roxy! Me and him are no longer together."

"Wow! He didn't tell me that!" Roxy said.

"He didn't tell us a lot of shit, Roxy. I don't have shit to say to him, like serious!" China stopped and became speechless when she saw the big-ass diamond on Roxy's hand.

"Bitch, what's wrong with you?" Roxy exclaimed.

"No, bitch! Where did you get that big-ass rock on your hand?" China replied, grabbing Roxy's hand to examine the ring.

"I'm engaged—and pregnant!" Roxy said with a smile on her face.

"Really?" China shrieked with excitement. "I'm going to be an auntie!" she added while hugging Roxy. "This is wonderful news."

"It's scary, though," Roxy confessed.

"Why is that?"

"Because I don't know what to expect. I'm about to be a mom," Roxy cried.

China hugged Roxy to comfort her. She understood what Roxy was going through from experiencing it herself.

"You'll do good, Roxy. There's no need to stress. It's not good for the baby," China warned her.

Roxy had no clue that China had just given up an innocent child for adoption. China had lost two kids in the same year, and now she found out that her man wasn't the man for her.

"Well, I have to get to work. We're holding a vigil for Jane at the restaurant tonight. Will you be there?" Roxy asked.

"I can't, Roxy. It's too much. Besides, I'm preparing to go out of town sooner than I expected," China told her.

"Okay, China. Well, call me when you sit down. I'll put some flowers down for you. It's a good thing that the kids weren't in the apartment," Roxy said.

"Yeah, that's a good thing," China said.

But I wouldn't have killed no kids, Sis! China reflected.

China watched Roxy leave, and then walked inside the house. Zorro met her at the door and jumped all over her.

"Hey there, boy!" China said, rubbing his head and pulling back his jaws.

China walked into the kitchen and got Zorro some fresh water and a fat bowl of chow. When she turned on her iPhone, she found a dozen missed calls, six from Smooth and the rest from Roxy.

* * *

Smooth was surprised to hear that Jane was murdered. He was perplexed trying to figure out who would have wanted her dead.

"Rosco, I just can't believe that she's dead. Maybe it's the Mexicans retaliating because they knew she was living in my apartment complex," Smooth said to Rosco, who was playing a close game of chess against Baby Dread.

"Why didn't they just burn the complex to the ground?" Rosco suggested.

"That does make sense. Any enemy would do that first if that was the case."

"Exactly, son," Rosco said as he made a move, putting Baby Dread in check. "Check!" Rosco shouted and signed to Baby Dread.

"Then, China's not picking up the phone either."

"She'll come through, mon. You were honest, and that's better than lying to her, mon, and having her find out on her own," Rosco suggested. "She'll realize that she can't stay mad, especially when you kept it honest," he added, speaking from experience.

Rosco had no knowledge of Smooth's HIV status. Smooth was afraid to tell him about what was going on. For if he did, a prudent man such as Rosco might have some different advice for him.

In fact, Smooth was still indecisive as to whether to he was going to reveal his status to China. Part of him wanted to be honest, but being honest about Amanda had gotten him in a bad situation with her. He could only imagine what her reaction would be when he told her that he had HIV.

"I'ma go try her again," Smooth said to Rosco as he strutted from the cell to the phone area.

He tried her number again, but he got the same number of rings and then it went to voicemail.

Damn it, China! Please pick up the damn phone! Smooth thought as he tried her again.

* * *

Money walked out of Jackson Memorial Hospital trying his best to bridle his emotions. But it was hard for him after seeing the plug get pulled on Choppa. Choppa's entire immediate family stood around his hospital bed and prayed before removing him from life support. His condition had worsened over the months. Money hopped in his Range Rover and checked the time. It was 8:30 p.m., and Tabby was attending her girl Jane's vigil.

This entire day is a mess! Money thought as he navigated out of the hospital parking lot.

Money's phone chimed, and he answered immediately. "Hello."

"What's up, Money? I need eight ounces," his client requested.

"Where you at?"

"27th."

"Give me thirty minutes," Money told him.

Money accelerated to the trap house to pick up the eight ounces. He never rode with drugs on him if he wasn't making a sell. Metro-Dade police stopped anyone and conducted illegal searches every day in Miami. When Money pulled up to the trap house, he quickly rushed inside, leaving his Range Rover running. He then grabbed eight ounces of crack cocaine and placed it inside a brown paper bag. When Money stepped outside and closed the door to lock it, he only heard the loud pop—and then he heard and saw nothing else. Money's body hit the ground, where his remaining brains poured from his head. Miguel looked at the front door and was thrilled as he stared at the blood splatter. He ran from the scene and hopped into the SUV where Marco was waiting on him. Money became an easy target after they spotted him a couple blocks back.

"One shot. Perfect kill, esé!" Miguel informed Marco.

"Good job, esé!" Marco congratulated Miguel.

"He never saw it coming."

"That's how it's supposed to be, homes," Marco said as he accelerated far away from the scene.

23

CHINA WAS ENJOYING Spencer's company on the road and was happy to get away from all the havoc in Miami. In the past two days after the death of Money, she had learned that Jane had AIDS, by watching the news and social media on Facebook. That news disturbed her and caused her to report to the first clinic to get tested. China's results came back in less than twenty-four hours, and she was negative for any STDs.

As a celebration, she called Spencer over, made him dinner, and led him to the bedroom, where they fucked all night long. When morning came, the duo was on the road traveling north on their way to New York. It was Saturday, and China made it to Lowell Correctional Institution just before 3:00 p.m. She had an hour to see Jenny, someone she was eager to visit.

"I won't be long. I'd rather stop now and drive all the way back with no stops," she said to Spencer as she unfastened her seatbelt.

"Take your time. I'll be here. I'm too far away to leave now," Spencer joked.

"You make me want to bring the keys with me," China said, looking at him.

"I'm only kidding. Go see ya girl!" he said as he leaned in and gave her a kiss. "That'll hold me down until you get back," Spencer said, tasting China's strawberry lip gloss.

"You're so crazy!"

"Yeah, about you!" Spencer joked.

After going through all the frisk procedures, China purchased an 18-wheeler and a cold Coke. Ten minutes later and Jenny showed up with a bright smile. She was so happy to see China. The first things she noticed were the scars on the bridge of her nose and upper lips.

"China, I'm so happy to see you," Jenny expressed as she embraced China and gave her a kiss.

"And I'm happy to see you too, baby," China replied. "Here, sit down and eat."

"Why so late?"

"I'ma be too busy to come by and see you on Sunday, so I stopped by while I was on my way," China explained.

"Let me guess. You're going to New York for Smooth again."

"Fuck Smooth! It's not even about him no more!" China said.

"What happened?" Jenny asked while chewing on her 18-wheeler sandwich.

"Too much shit—" China choked on her tears "—to take him back."

China then wiped away the stream of tears that fell from her eyes.

Jenny was hurt seeing China cry in front of her. Had she been able to imagine the pain that China was going through, Jenny wouldn't have understood how to deal with the problem herself.

"Tell me everything!" Jenny said.

For fifteen minutes, China explained everything to Jenny, including discovering that Jane had AIDS. She could trust Jenny with her life, and she realized that coming to see her was what she needed. China was very surprised to see Jenny's calm reaction when she informed her about Spencer.

"You have to leave Smooth, China. What if he has it too?"

"I won't give him a chance to give it to me," China replied.

"What are you going to do?"

"I'ma free him and then kill him."

"He's not worth it! Stick with Spencer," Jenny suggested.

"Spencer's—" China got stuck trying to describe her and his sudden relationship "—he's just a play toy!"

"Our play toy?" Jenny inquired.

"Our play toy," China assured her.

"Visitation is now over, everyone," the CO announced over the PA system.

* * *

"Mmmm, yes, daddy!" a crackhead trick named Peaches moaned out as Ham fucked her hard from the back.

He pounded away at her stank pussy with no mercy in his strokes.

"Yes, Ham! Mmmm, shit! Beat this pussy up, daddy!"

"Arrgghh, shit!" Ham growled, pulling his dick out of Peaches and shooting his load onto her back and skinny ass cheeks.

Peaches turned around and placed Ham's dick inside her mouth while she sucked him off until he was dry. When Ham heard someone knocking at the door, he quickly put on some pants, grabbed his Glock .40 from the nightstand, and looked at Peaches.

"I'll be back. Get a hit ready for us," he ordered her.

"Okay, daddy!"

Ham walked out of the room and to the front door. Without looking through the peephole, Ham opened the door and saw a man standing there who he had never seen before.

"Who are you? It looks like you're lost," Ham said.

"I'm your new neighbor," the stranger said before he caught Ham with a nimble two-piece to his jaw, knocking him out.

Ham stood for a second before he collapsed to the ground. Tic walked inside the apartment and closed the door. He knew where to find the trick who he had seen Ham bring back. Tic walked to the bedroom where he found her smoking from the crack pipe. When she looked up and saw Tic with a gun aimed at her, she tried to scream but was stopped by Tic's slugs.

Boom! Boom! Boom!

Tic shot the trick dead. He then walked back into the living room and handcuffed Ham and waited for his boss to show up.

* * *

China would never guess that she and Spencer were cuddling each other at the same hotel that Smooth had brought Amanda to when he had taken the same trip. China and Spencer had ordered some delicious Chinese food and watched a horror movie. The movie was coming to an end, and it was almost time for China to go meet with Jefe for the last time. Before she left Spencer at the hotel, she wanted to melt into his arms. China allowed him to hold her from behind while watching the movie. With one turn, China was face-to-face with him.

She placed her mouth to his and climbed on top of him, kissing him deeply and passionately. Spencer's hands caressed her body and pulled down her satin thong. China slid down Spencer's body, planting kisses along the way. When she got to his bulging cock, she pulled down his briefs and began to stroke his enormous cock. She had never seen herself being with a white man, but she was grateful that her first one proved to be a champion in the sack. China placed Spencer's cock in her mouth and gave him some slow head while massaging his balls. The feeling was great to Spencer. He had experienced unique oral sex from call girls since he had been in Miami, but he never felt a connection and affection like China was causing him. His toes curled, and his ass cheeks tightened, causing him to moan out China's name. "Damn, China. You're the best!"

China didn't want to bring Spencer to his peak too fast. She was on a timeframe and wanted to feel him deep in her world before she had to go. China stopped sucking his dick and climbed on top of him and straddled him. She reached behind her with one hand and grabbed Spencer's wet cock. She slowly guided his dick into her wet pussy and rocked back and forth. Each time she came down, she filled her pussy with more of his cock.

"Spencer! This dick is so good!"

"Take your time, beautiful! You feel good to me, China!" Spencer complimented her as he began sucking on her nipples.

China began to increase her pace once she became accustomed to his cock, which is just what she wanted.

"Spencer! Fuck me, baby!" China demanded.

Spencer wasted no time flipping her onto her back while his cock stayed inside her.

He pulled back until just his head was in her pussy, and then he slammed his entire cock deep inside her.

"Mmmm, shit!" she purred loudly.

"This what you want?"

"Yes, Spencer! Fuck me baby!" China screamed loud enough for the neighbors to hear.

* * *

Smooth was stressing badly from not hearing anything from China. If he had hair, he would have been pulling it by now. Rosco tried all he could to help Smooth out with comforting advice, but it seemed like it went in one ear and out the other. Smooth was walking to the phones when two sergeants walked into the dorm looking directly at him.

"Mr. Johnson, could you please come with us? You have someone here to see you," one of the sergeants stated.

It's the health department, Smooth thought as he walked off with them.

When Smooth stepped into the main hallway of the jail, another one of the sergeants cuffed him in the front and then led the way. Smooth noticed that they were not heading to the medical unit when they passed by it, so he became curious. "Where am I going?"

"You're going to see a pit bull in a skirt," the sergeant informed Smooth, who had completely missed the dog reference.

He didn't find it humorous and remained quiet. A minute later, Smooth was being led into a small interview room.

"Sit down at the table. Your guest will be here shortly," the sergeant said.

Smooth sat down at the table and waited for thirty minutes before the door opened. When he looked back and saw the black detective, his heart dropped. He smelled trouble, but he didn't know from which angle it was coming.

"Hello, Donavan Smooth Johnson. My name is Agent Debra Jones, and I'm the head of the DEA," she introduced herself, standing on the opposite side of the table. She then slid over a copy of his indictment. "DEA of Miami, Smooth, and we've been looking for you day and night, sir," she said to him as she sat down at the table.

Smooth looked at the highlighted charges and instantly became angry. He was staring at a long list of charges, from first-degree murder of multiple Mexicans to drug affiliation. They were even charging him with Juan's and Tracy's murders, even though he knew China killed her. It gave him confidence because he knew that he was nowhere near the scene.

It takes evidence to convict someone, Smooth remembered Rosco's advice.

Smooth smiled and caused Agent Jones to explode.

"So you find this shit funny, Donavan, huh? Well, we'll see how funny it is when Miami hands you a life sentence, Smooth!"

"Woman, whoever the hell you are, I don't see nothing in Miami. These bogus charges are a damn scam. I have my lawyer. Do y'all have a court date?" Smooth said.

"Yeah, we do. And we have our reliable CIs who will gladly take the stand against you," Agent Jones said as she stood up and walked toward the door. "I'm going to give you time to think about cooperating. We want the man who put you on your high horse, Smooth," Agent Jones said as she left the interrogation room.

Pit bull in a skirt. She sure does look like one! Smooth thought.

They wanted Jefe, someone who Smooth would never give them.

As he was being led back to his dorm, he thought about the mess he was in. He now had more than Ham to worry about.

Someone in Miami is talking, and they are close to my operation, Smooth thought. *I can't believe this shit. China, I need you, damn it! Stop being so adamant!* Smooth thought as he walked back into the dorm.

* * *

It was 1:30 a.m. when China and Spencer arrived in Martin County. Spencer pulled into the apartment complex and killed the lights.

"Are you ready for this?" Spencer asked.

"Does it look like I'm not?" China replied.

"That's what I'm talking about, you feisty chick!" Spencer said, causing China to chuckle.

"You're crazy boy! Now let's get this job done!" she said.

Spencer led the way while China followed him to the apartment with a duffel bag in her hand. They both wore gloves to carry out the task that they were there to handle.

When they stood in front of apartment 305, Spencer knocked twice. A moment went by before the door opened, and Spencer and China were staring at Tic.

"Welcome, boss!" Tic said as he stepped aside to let them inside.

Once they were all inside, they locked the door behind them. The reek of decomposition strongly lingered in the air.

"Damn! Did you do our job already?" China asked Tic.

"Nah! That's the crackhead trick he had keeping him company," Tic informed. "He's in the kitchen," he directed the duo while walking toward the kitchen.

When Spencer and China entered the small kitchen, they found Ham strapped to the kitchen table, handcuffed in the back. China walked up to him and looked him in his eyes.

"What did he do with her?" China asked while checking the ropes that held down Ham.

"He chopped her up and saved her in the deep freezer," Tic informed China.

"Wow, that's smart!" China said as she spun around and looked at Spencer.

"It's your show, baby," Spencer said as he leaned against the refrigerator.

"At least give me a hand with the water hose," China requested.

"Sure," Spencer agreed as he took the duffel bag from China.

Spencer removed a green hose from the bag and connected it to a faucet in the utility closet above the washing machine. China looked at Ham with a towel in her hand and spoke: "I'ma need you to be honest with me. Do you understand me?"

Ham was unable to speak from the duct tape on his mouth, so he nodded his head yes.

"Okay, why did you turn on Smooth? You do know who Smooth is, right?" China said.

Ham nodded his head yes.

"Ready?" Spencer shouted to China.

China cut off the circulation to the hose so that the water wouldn't come pouring out.

"Yes, go ahead," China said.

The water came on, and she laid the towel over Ham's face. She then released the grip on the hose and let the water pour out onto Ham's face.

"We call this waterboarding," China said as she let the water run over Ham's face, who began wiggling and trying to avoid the torture of the water that made him feel like he was drowning.

Spencer and Tic stood back and enjoyed a good laugh as they watched the show. Ten minutes had passed before China stopped the circulation of the hose. She pulled the wet towel from Ham's face and then snatched the duct tape covering his mouth. Ham gasped for air, feeling like he was about to die.

"They made me tell on him! I swear I have no intentions of testifying against him!" Ham exclaimed.

"Did you act alone?"

"What?" Ham asked China.

"Do you have a snitch co-defendant, muthafucka?" China shouted before she slapped the shit out of Ham.

"No! No! I don't have no codefendant. I'm not going to…"

Before Ham could complete his plea, China covered his face with the towel and released the pressure on the water hose again, letting the water run onto Ham's face. The second wiggling round was worse for him, since he couldn't keep his mouth closed to prevent water from seeping inside. He began choking and drowning on the water. The straps that bound him to the table prevented him from turning his head. Before Ham drowned, China removed the towel and cut off the circulation once again. As Ham gasped for air and choked on water, China shoved the water hose down Ham's throat and released the pressure.

Damn! Spencer thought as he watched China drown Ham.

After two minutes with the hose down his throat, Ham's wiggling came to a halt.

"He looks dead to me. Tic, get rid of him," Spencer said as Tic began chopping Ham up with an ax.

Spencer and China left the apartment together, satisfied with how things turned out. As they were pulling out of the complex, Spencer's curiosity got the best of him, and China just knew that he would ask.

"Where did you learn to waterboard?"

China looked over at him and smiled. "YouTube. Now let's find us a room. I want to rest before the sun comes up," she said.

* * *

Smooth awoke out of his sleep when the cell door rolled back. It was after 8:00 a.m., the second roll out for the day. He did his routine hygiene and then dug into his locker for something to eat. As he reached for a honey bun, he heard a click from his cell speaker.

"Inmate Johnson, you have a visit at booth 24."

Smooth's stomach quickly formed butterflies. He knew that it couldn't be anyone but China. He was excited, yet he was still undecided whether to tell her of his status or not. Smooth walked out of the dorm to the visitation room. There weren't many visitors since it was so early in the morning.

When Smooth got to booth 24, he saw China smiling bright and looking real good.

Damn! She's beautiful, Smooth thought as he sat down and picked up the phone. "What's up, baby?"

"A lot is up, Smooth. I just hope that you can be a man and keep it real. Because when I leave here with the wrong answer, consider me out of your life forever, Smooth!" she said as she stared at him and noticed the stitches on his lips. "And it looks like someone beat your ass, nigga!"

"Yeah!" Smooth said and then sighed. "Listen, China. I kept it real with you about Amanda."

"Nigga, I'm not talking about no Amanda. I'm talking about this!" China said as she held up the letter that he had written to Jane.

Shit! Smooth thought, realizing at the same time that China killed Jane.

He had heard what the media was saying about Jane by Sue Rabbit, and he had no doubt in his mind that China knew as well.

I gotta keep it real; there's no way out! Smooth thought as tears cascaded down his face.

"China, I fucked up bad. She came on to me, and I fell for the bait instead of standing strong on my love for you."

"Did you use protection?" China asked.

Smooth swayed his head, and instantly China broke down.

"Smooth, you could have killed me! How could you do this?" China shrilled.

"China, you're okay. I seriously doubt that you're infected with anything."

"And what about you, Smooth, huh? Could you say the same? Look at you. You've lost a tremendous amount of weight."

"That's because I have HIV, China. I'm sorry. I know I fucked up, but please don't come up here making my life any more miserable than it already is. Woman, there's nothing I could possibly say that'll take back the hurt I've caused us both."

He's pouring his heart out. He's hurt, China realized as the tears cascaded down her face.

"China, you have a chance to live your life. I've killed myself trying to cheat life!"

"Don't feel like that, Smooth. We could have been friends," China said, not believing what she was saying.

At that moment, she realized just how much she loved him in spite of his cheating and the revelation of his new status.

"I love you, China. But I will never see them streets again, and I will never harm you," he said.

"That problem you had is gone, Smooth. It's handled. You're coming home."

"No, China. The DEA from Miami paid a visit yesterday, and I'm charged with Juan's and Tracy's murders."

"But you didn't do it," China said.

"We know this," Smooth replied, "but the other charges, they have an unknown CI. Someone in Miami is talking."

"Smooth, why didn't you just let the game go? None of this shit would be happening," China said.

"I'm sorry, China. I fucked up!"

"I got to give it to you. At least you didn't try to justify this letter. You know we can't be together, Smooth, but I'm not just gonna leave you out to dry. If you have to do some time, I'll sell your house and send you the money. But as of now, I just want to distance myself from you, Smooth. I'm seeing someone else, and I want to focus on what we're developing."

Smooth couldn't believe what he was hearing. Someone had stolen his childhood sweetheart, and he couldn't even be mad. When Smooth spoke, he spoke genuinely from the heart. "I love you, China. What makes you happy makes me happy."

"I love you too, Smooth," China said as she hung up the phone and left the visiting room, with no intentions of ever returning.

Smooth sat at the booth and felt relieved from all the stress and pressure that he was going through. He now just had to get used to being alone, and honest if he ever encountered another woman.

I wonder who the lucky individual is? Whoever he is, he's a lucky person, Smooth thought.

24

One Week Later

CHINA AND SPENCER were having the time of their lives with each other. Spencer had practically moved in with China and Zorro, being that he was home with her every night. China had opened up to Spencer about everything the night they had returned from Miami. It was evident that the visit wasn't an ordinary one, from her muteness on the drive back. When they arrived in Miami at China's place, Spencer offered her his support through whatever mental dysfunction she was going through. The bombshell she dropped on him was not what he had expected to hear. Spencer realized immediately after listening to China that he was the new lucky man. He had promised China that he would do his best to keep her happy, and that's all China needed to hear.

Every morning she expected to receive a call from Smooth because she still loved him for being honest about his status. When she had mustered the might to tell Roxy, Roxy cried. Roxy and Smooth were close, and it hurt her to hear that Smooth was HIV positive. But for the most part, she was glad to hear that China wasn't infected and that she had found a new love—a love that surprised her, since Spencer was a white man.

As China emerged from the Jacuzzi, relaxing with a bottle of Dom Pérignon, she heard her phone ring. Her first thought was that it was Spencer calling to inform her that he was on his way. It was 8:00 p.m., and she had been relaxing in the

Jacuzzi for two hours now. When China picked up her phone and checked the caller ID, she saw that it was Sue Rabbit.

"What's up, bro?" China answered.

"Please tell me that you haven't put your guns on the shelf," Sue Rabbit said.

China looked at her nightstand and saw her two Glock .40s sitting side by side.

"Why would I do that? What's up?" China asked, wrapping herself in a towel and then sitting on the edge of the bed.

"I got a call from Mac, and he tells me that our boy Mario and his men just stepped through the door at Club Rage. Daddy Yanky is in town, and Pitbull is expected to show up as a surprise guest," Sue Rabbit explained.

The news was music to China's ears, and her blood was already pumping. She couldn't miss the opportunity to kill her biggest enemy.

"Where are you?" China asked Sue Rabbit.

"I'm on my way to you now."

"Go to the club and wait until I get there," China said.

"Okay."

With trembling hands, China called Spencer's phone and got him on the second ring.

"What's up, beautiful?" Spencer answered.

"Baby, where are you?" China asked, with extreme excitement in her voice.

"What's the matter?"

"Club Rage. Mario is there with his men!"

"So what are your plans, baby?" Spencer asked.

"What do you mean, Spencer? Where are you?"

"I'm on my way to you. Am I making a blank trip?"

"No, come and hurry. We need to get over to the club," China said and then hung up.

She then called Sue Rabbit back again.

"Hello," Sue Rabbit answered.

"How much are the tickets?"

"We're already taken care of. When you pull up, come to the back and call me," Sue informed her.

"Okay, bro. See you soon," China said before she hung up the phone.

"It's going to be a cold day in hell before I miss this muthafucka!" China said as she got dressed in suitable attire for the task that lay ahead of her.

* * *

Mario and Javier were enjoying themselves in the VIP room with all the pretty Latinas. The club was packed with M-13s who were happy to see Mario out having a good time with them. Since Juan's death, the M-13s had only seen Mario a couple times, and he was always in a hurry to return to his low-key spot. Daddy Yanky was his favorite Latino rapper, and he couldn't miss his performance for nothing in the world.

"Esé! Do you want another bottle? I'm going for one!" Javier told Mario, who was dancing with a gorgeous but barely-legal five foot two Mexican chica.

"Yeah, esé! I think I'ma book us a private VIP room with this bonita!" Mario shouted over the loud music in the club.

"This is top notch, homie. If we want privacy, we will take mama and her friend to a motel," Javier shouted to Mario in Spanish.

The Mexican woman smiled at Javier and blew him a kiss.

"Me and my girl would love to join you two after the club!" she said to Javier and Mario. "The only problem is I ride solo, so it'll only be us three, and me phat pussy," the Mexican chica said as she snatched the bottle of champagne from Mario's hand and killed what was left in it. "We need another bottle," she said as she handed it to Javier.

Javier smiled at the Mexican woman and then strutted off past Marco and Miguel, who were having a splendid time with some chicas on the dance floor.

Damn, I have to piss! Javier said to himself as he moved through the crowd.

Javier quickly weighed his options: the bar or restroom. He chose the restroom. When he walked past a garbage can, he dumped the empty bottles of champagne and walked down the hallway to the restrooms, where a couple of his brothers were inside snorting cocaine and smoking pot. Javier never saw the threat on his trail. The only person who did spot the threat was Marco, who expected it to show up. Marco wasn't naive; no Latino concert stopped an American from attending.

* * *

China watched from the camera room as Spencer followed Javier to the restroom at a safe distance. At the same time, China kept a close eye on Mario, who looked like a completely different man than the one in his mug shot. When China looked at the floor camera, she saw a familiar-looking Mexican man looking down the hallway of the restroom.

"Mac, can you zoom in on this guy?" China asked him.

Mac tapped the keyboard twice, which controlled the monitor, and immediately had a close-up view of her. Flashes of the driver when she was attacked appeared in her head.

"It's him!" she said. "And he sees Spencer. He knows Spencer's the man who he was in a shootout with," China said as she racked her Uzi .22 and pulled down her ski mask.

China was in the same hallway as Spencer. When she looked at the monitor, Javier had entered the restroom, while Spencer was about ten feet away with Marco creeping up on him with a knife in his hand.

With amazing speed, China stepped out into the hallway and aimed at Spencer's chest. "Duck!" she shouted.

When Spencer ducked, China pulled the trigger to her Uzi and hit Marco head-on in his torso with a storm of bullets. The shots rang out loud. And though they were in a club surrounded by M-13s, they had the advantage of having weapons. Everyone else had been checked for weapons before entering the club.

When Spencer turned around, Marco was still breathing. The music on the dance floor had drowned out the sounds of the gunshots, and the people in the restroom mistook the shots as an imitation of gunshots on a track.

"Fucker! Tried to sneak up on me, huh?" Spencer shouted as he pulled out his two Glock .50s and stood over Marco.

Spencer instantly recognized Marco and pumped two shots into his face as China ran up to him.

"Baby, the restroom. Let's go!" she said as she pulled Spencer away from a dead Marco.

Together, the duo ran into the restroom and startled everyone. China let her Uzi bark while Spencer let both Glocks get to work. There were twelve Mexican men, and the duo took down the whole dozen. However, Javier was not in the count.

China and Spencer looked at each other and then over at the stalls. China backed up to the door and then squatted while aiming underneath the stalls. She saw no feet. Spencer kicked in each door while China aimed, ready to hit their target. When the duo got to the last stall, Spencer kicked the door in and felt a sharp object catch him in his neck. China squeezed the trigger and shot Javier with a storm of bullets, causing his body to sit on the toilet. Behind him was a splattered wall of blood. China looked at Spencer and almost fainted when she saw his blood-covered hands. She looked back at Javier and hit him twice more in the head. Javier was a perfect darter and had won a good shot at Spencer.

"Baby, we got to get you out of here!" China said to Spencer, who couldn't talk.

The knife landed perfectly through his larynx. When Spencer took two steps, he collapsed to his knees while staring up at China, who immediately began to cry.

"Go!" Spencer managed to let out.

China pulled out her iPhone and called Sue Rabbit.

"Yo!"

"Spencer's down. Let's do this shit and go!" China ordered as she watched Spencer fall to the ground before she could catch him. "No, baby. Please don't do this!" China cried as she heard the club go into frantic mode at the sound of the gunshots.

China saw that Spencer's eyes were wide open. She knew that he was dead and that there was no need to check for assurance.

"I love your crazy ass!" China yelled before she ran out of the restroom toward the VIP room where Sue Rabbit and Tic had Mario cornered.

"We finally meet, huh?" China shouted at Mario, who looked fearless and prepared to die.

Tic and Sue Rabbit never saw Miguel, who had crept back inside the club with his MAC-10. Their only focus was to kill Mario and make their exit out the back door, the same way they had entered.

"Bitch! Do you think you put fear in Mario?" Mario said to China as he boldly began walking toward her like a fearless man.

He didn't make it past Sue Rabbit, who cracked Mario in his face with the butt of his AK-47, knocking him to the ground.

China walked up and stood over him with her Uzi. She lifted up her ski mask to let Mario see her face. "Remember me in hell!" she shouted as she squeezed the trigger, filling Mario's body with a storm of bullets.

When Sue Rabbit looked out onto the dance floor, he spotted Miguel at the bar, aiming at China. Before Sue could raise his gun, Miguel squeezed off, rapidly hitting China multiple times.

"Nooooo!" Sue Rabbit screamed as he squeezed the trigger of his AK-47 and hit Miguel in his face, sending a spray of blood everywhere, along with his body flying backward behind the bar.

"Shit!" Sue Rabbit exclaimed as he made a dash toward China.

He was happy to see her eyes still open and that she was still breathing.

"Tic, help me get her out of here! Get her gun and cover me!" Sue Rabbit ordered Tic, who did as he was told.

Tic wanted to get out alive just as much as Sue Rabbit did, so he decided to follow the prudent man in the crazy situation. Sue picked China up into his arms and carried her down the hall toward the back door while Tic watched their backs.

"It's burning, Sue."

"Don't talk, China. Please let me get you out of here. You'll be okay. Let me talk, not you!" Sue Rabbit told her as he carried her out the back door with the help of Mac, who had come out of the camera room with the keys to unlock the back door.

"Tic, drive us to the hospital. No red lights. Go ninety miles per hour, man. She's losing too much blood," Sue Rabbit shouted as he climbed into the backseat of his Range Rover with China. "Be a good, strong girl and hold on for me, China!" he said to her.

China smiled at his words of encouragement.

She was in too much pain to speak what was on her mind.

Tic had the pedal to the metal, nonchalantly running through red lights like Sue Rabbit had instructed him.

"It's so cold, Sue. Cut off the AC," China said in pain as she felt her body get extremely cold.

Sue Rabbit looked at the AC and saw that it was off. "Damn it, China! Stop talking!"

"Cold, Sue. I can't see you!" China could barely get out.

"I got you. I'm here, China. We're almost there, okay!"

"Tell Roxy, GaGa, and Smooth that I love them, please."

When Sue Rabbit looked down at China's hand and saw the strength leave it, he knew that she had died in his arms. "China, hold on! We're almost there!" Sue Rabbit said to her, even though she was no longer with him.

Sue Rabbit knew it, but he didn't want to believe it. China had just taken her last breath.

"Damn, China!" Sue Rabbit cried as he closed her eyes and kissed her on her forehead. "Rest in peace, sister-in-law," he said as Tic pulled into Jackson Memorial Hospital.

EPILOGUE

Five Years Later

ROXY AND SUE Rabbit were celebrating the anniversary of China's death, like they had been doing every year since she passed. It was free food day at all their restaurants throughout Dade and Broward Counties. Roxy had opened six restaurants with the help of Sue Rabbit. The couple had married and now had two beautiful girls a year apart named Taneshia and Chinetta.

Taneshia was the eldest and strongly favored her Auntie China. And from what GaGa could remember of China when she was a baby, Taneshia acted just like her auntie. Sue Rabbit had given up the streets and helped his wife's business do major numbers. Everyone was still trying to get used to China being gone, including Smooth, who was serving a harsh seventy-five years in a federal prison. He had no chance when Big Mitch boldly testified against him. Consequently, Big Mitch was killed in a home invasion months later.

Sue Rabbit and Roxy kept Smooth's inmate account full and had been to visit him a couple times over the years, having to travel by plane since he was stationed in Virginia. In spite of Money's death leaving Tabby alone as a single mother, Roxy made her a manager over the restaurant in Hollywood, Florida, where she lived with her little boy, who was the spit and image of Money.

"Mrs. Jackson, these ribs are delicious," a teenaged black girl complimented.

"Thank that man over there on the grill," Roxy said, pointing to her husband working on the enormous grill.

"I will, Mrs. Jackson," the girl said as she strutted off to thank Sue Rabbit, who had a line of people waiting to get their BBQ ribs fresh off the grill.

* * *

Jenny was out of prison enjoying her freedom and living in Orlando. The death of China broke her down and transformed her, but with the help of Carlisha, Jenny got through her grief and restored a sane mind. She was working at one of Roxy's restaurants in Miami on the weekends as an assistant manager while working weekdays at a gym in Orlando. The day Jenny received the letter from Roxy offering her a job once she was released from prison, had moved her.

In spite of her sexuality, Jenny had found a loving and caring man in Orlando who was ready for Carlisha to be released to join their relationship. In remembrance of China, Jenny purchased an expensive tattoo of China's portrait on her right breast. Not a day went by, despite her newfound happiness, that Jenny didn't think about her. But deep down in her heart, Jenny hated Smooth. She blamed him for China dying at the hands of his enemies.

Amanda was now living in Atlanta and working at an alternative school for misbehaved young females. She was a counselor who informed the young females of the dangers of going astray. She was honest about her HIV status and used herself as an example of having unprotected sex. She had all the money a person could ever desire, but no amount could cure her virus. Young people, the last thing that Amanda would have ever expected was for a childhood sweetheart to stray from his beloved sweetheart and affect her with HIV.

BOOKS BY GOOD2GO AUTHORS

GOOD 2 GO FILMS PRESENTS

**THE HAND I WAS DEALT- FREE WEB SERIES
NOW AVAILABLE ON YOUTUBE!
YOUTUBE.COM/SILKWHITE212**

SEASON TWO NOW AVAILABLE

To order books, please fill out the order form below:

To order films please go to www.good2gofilms.com

Name:_____

Address:_____

City: _____ State: _____ Zip Code: _____

Phone:_____

Email:_____

Method of Payment: Check   VISA   MASTERCARD

Credit Card#:_____

Name as it appears on card: _____

Signature: _____

Item Name	Price	Qty	Amount
48 Hours to Die – Silk White	$14.99		
A Hustler's Dream - Ernest Morris	$14.99		
A Hustler's Dream 2 - Ernest Morris	$14.99		
Business Is Business – Silk White	$14.99		
Business Is Business 2 – Silk White	$14.99		
Business Is Business 3 – Silk White	$14.99		
Childhood Sweethearts – Jacob Spears	$14.99		
Childhood Sweethearts 2 – Jacob Spears	$14.99		
Childhood Sweethearts 3 - Jacob Spears	$14.99		
Childhood Sweethearts 4 - Jacob Spears	$14.99		
Flipping Numbers – Ernest Morris	$14.99		
Flipping Numbers 2 – Ernest Morris	$14.99		
He Loves Me, He Loves You Not - Mychea	$14.99		
He Loves Me, He Loves You Not 2 - Mychea	$14.99		
He Loves Me, He Loves You Not 3 - Mychea	$14.99		
He Loves Me, He Loves You Not 4 – Mychea	$14.99		
He Loves Me, He Loves You Not 5 – Mychea	$14.99		
Lord of My Land – Jay Morrison	$14.99		
Lost and Turned Out – Ernest Morris	$14.99		
Married To Da Streets – Silk White	$14.99		
M.E.R.C. - Make Every Rep Count Health and Fitness	$14.99		
My Besties – Asia Hill	$14.99		
My Besties 2 – Asia Hill	$14.99		
My Besties 3 – Asia Hill	$14.99		
My Besties 4 – Asia Hill	$14.99		
My Boyfriend's Wife - Mychea	$14.99		
My Boyfriend's Wife 2 – Mychea	$14.99		
Naughty Housewives – Ernest Morris	$14.99		
Naughty Housewives 2 – Ernest Morris	$14.99		
Naughty Housewives 3 – Ernest Morris	$14.99		

Never Be The Same – Silk White	$14.99		
Stranded – Silk White	$14.99		
Slumped – Jason Brent	$14.99		
Tears of a Hustler - Silk White	$14.99		
Tears of a Hustler 2 - Silk White	$14.99		
Tears of a Hustler 3 - Silk White	$14.99		
Tears of a Hustler 4- Silk White	$14.99		
Tears of a Hustler 5 – Silk White	$14.99		
Tears of a Hustler 6 – Silk White	$14.99		
The Panty Ripper - Reality Way	$14.99		
The Panty Ripper 3 – Reality Way	$14.99		
The Solution – Jay Morrison	$14.99		
The Teflon Queen – Silk White	$14.99		
The Teflon Queen 2 – Silk White	$14.99		
The Teflon Queen 3 – Silk White	$14.99		
The Teflon Queen 4 – Silk White	$14.99		
The Teflon Queen 5 – Silk White	$14.99		
The Teflon Queen 6 - Silk White	$14.99		
The Vacation – Silk White	$14.99		
Tied To A Boss - J.L. Rose	$14.99		
Tied To A Boss 2 - J.L. Rose	$14.99		
Tied To A Boss 3 - J.L. Rose	$14.99		
Time Is Money - Silk White	$14.99		
Two Mask One Heart – Jacob Spears and Trayvon Jackson	$14.99		
Two Mask One Heart 2 – Jacob Spears and Trayvon Jackson	$14.99		
Two Mask One Heart 3 – Jacob Spears and Trayvon Jackson	$14.99		
Young Goonz – Reality Way	$14.99		
Young Legend – J.L. Rose	$14.99		
Subtotal:			
Tax:			
Shipping (Free) U.S. Media Mail:			
Total:			

Make Checks Payable To:
Good2Go Publishing
7311 W Glass Lane,
Laveen, AZ 85339